TAKING THE LEAD

Stephanie Perry Moore
&
Derrick Moore

TAKING THE LEAD

Alec London Series
Book 5

MOODY PUBLISHERS
CHICAGO

Edited by Kathryn Hall
Interior design: Ragont Design
Cover design: TS Design Studio
Cover photo and illustrations: TS Design Studio and 123rf.com

Library of Congress Cataloging-in-Publication Data

Moore, Stephanie Perry.
    Taking the lead / Stephanie Perry Moore and Derrick Moore.
        p. cm. -- (Alec London series ; bk. #5)
    Summary: Alec is excited about being elected 5th grade class president and joining the track team, but when his grandmother's cancer gets worse, everything falls apart until he volunteers with a Special Olympics team and realizes that if disabled children can cope, so can he.
    ISBN 978-0-8024-0413-8
    [1. Conduct of life—Fiction. 2.Track and field—Fiction. 3. Sick—Fiction. 4. Special Olympics—Fiction 5. Christian life—Fiction. 6. African Americans—Fiction.] I. Moore, Derrick C. II. Title.
PZ7.M788125Tak 2012
[Fic]—dc23

                                                                2011041994

Printed by Bethany Press in Bloomington, MN - 02/2012

1 3 5 7 9 10 8 6 4 2

Printed in the United States of America

To our Godsons,
Danton Lynn, Dakari Jones
& Dorian Lee

We are so pleased with all of your accomplishments.
The Lord has given you all talents and you are soaring.
Though we haven't been with you
physically every step of the way,
Know that you are covered with our prayers.
Also we pray that you and every
reader will lead God's way!

Remember your godparents are cheering for you as you
successfully run the race of life . . . we love you!

Contents

True Winner

1

Standing in front of the class with a wide grin on her face, we could feel Dr. Richardson's excitement when she asked the big question, "Okay, class, who is going to be the next fifth-grade class president?"

Morgan was smiling from ear to ear. Trey was beaming as if he could see himself in the White House. Even Tyrod was excited, thinking maybe he had a chance. They could have it. I had no interest in running for any kind of office.

"First, we're going to lunch and then out for recess. Later, when we come back, we'll take a vote. Remember, only one person from our class can put his or her name on the ballot with the nominees from the other classes. So really think hard about who you want to elect to represent the entire fifth-grade class."

During lunch, I was eating my cheeseburger when I noticed all my friends looking over at me. They were sitting across the table, smiling and whispering like they had some kind of plan.

It wasn't just Morgan and Trey, but Zarick was sitting with us. To have Zarick in on something with my buddies was very interesting because the two of us had just become friends.

You see, he had been picking on me since school started, following his buddy Tyrod's direction. Then, after we found out Tyrod was stirring up trouble on purpose, Zarick and I actually got to know each other. Tyrod wasn't happy about it because he didn't want the two of us to be friends.

Anyway, I was really glad to see Zarick in school. Last weekend, he called and told me there was trouble at his home. As it turned out, his mother's boyfriend was being abusive. I told my father what was going on and Dad called the police. Thankfully, the police and fire department got there just in time.

Seeing Zarick with a smile on his face made me jump right into a conversation with him about how things were going.

"So everything's good?"

I didn't want to be fake or phony, but I had to take the lead in this conversation. It was important for me to make sure my friend was okay. Ever since we became friends, Zarick had made me promise not to tell anyone about his situation. But when I found out how bad the problem was, I couldn't keep that promise. Once it was all over, he told me it was all right that I told my dad.

I was super glad that I did too, because when we got to his house, it was in flames. My heart stopped for a minute when I saw that scene, but thankfully his family was okay. Still, that didn't necessarily mean everything was all right with him.

When Zarick was taking too long to give me an answer, I said, "So talk to me! Tell me, what's up?"

He leaned in and said in a low voice, "Everything's good, thanks to you, Alec. I'm really glad you said something. My mom told me that I can always talk to her, but I wasn't saying anything because I thought she was happy with that guy. She said that I should come to her from now on with my concerns. My mom definitely wants to know if someone is mistreating me or my sister."

It all sounded good to me. Then Zarick hesitated a second and added, "BUT . . . we may have to move."

"Huh?" I said, hearing what I didn't want to hear.

"She's not sure yet. We might go and live with my grandmother."

"Where is that?"

"In Macon, Georgia," Zarick replied. I could tell he wasn't too happy about it either. "It's an hour from here," he added.

Just when I made a new friend, I might lose that new friend. Not cool. But I guess it was a fair trade-off if Zarick, his mom, and little sister were going to be safe.

"So enough about all that," Zarick said to me, smiling again. "What are you gonna do?"

"I'm gonna finish eatin'," I responded. But I wasn't really clear on exactly what he meant.

"Oh, so now you got jokes?" Zarick said, giving me a smirk. "You should be the nominee from our class tomorrow. You'd make a great fifth-grade class president."

"Huh?" I replied. He might as well have been speaking a foreign language. "Why would you say that?"

"Because you care about others, you're smart, and you're cool. If I do get to stay here, I want the fifth-grade activities at the end of this year to be really slammin'. Last year's class didn't do anything, and everybody said it was because they didn't have good planning. I don't want that to be the case for us. We've waited a long time to be in the fifth grade. Now that we're here, we should have a big celebration."

Morgan and Trey kept on eating and didn't say a word. I guess they thought Zarick was doing a pretty good job of trying to convince me.

Actually, he was right. I remember two years ago when my brother, Antoine, was in the fifth grade, they did a lot of stuff. They had a whole week of celebration, and it ended with them going to Six Flags. Antoine wasn't the class president, but he bragged a lot about the people who helped put it all together.

But me? Running for office? No way. I wasn't interested and that's exactly what I told Zarick.

"If I didn't think I might have to move, I would do it," Zarick said, looking at me. I could tell he was still trying to challenge me.

Because I wanted him to stick around, I responded,

"Oh, man, that's a good idea! Maybe you should talk to your mom about it. That way, if you get the position, you won't have to move."

"Boy, please, like me bein' fifth-grade class president is gonna keep food on our table. Just run already, Alec."

About twenty minutes later, we were outside on the playground. Morgan and Trey still had sly looks on their faces. When they approached me, it was about the very same thing.

"I still don't understand why you won't run, Alec," Trey said, after I repeated the same answer I gave Zarick.

"Like I've been sayin', I don't want to," I added, with as much emphasis as I could gather. Then I asked bluntly, "Why don't you run?"

Looking me square in the eyes, Trey said, "Because I won't win. You're the one who can get the support of all the fifth-grade classes. We're askin' you to do it. If you're the leader, we can get behind you and help make this year great."

Not being able to come up with another excuse, I turned to my other friend and said, "Morgan, all the classes would support you too."

"No, there are some girls in those other classes who roll their eyes at me every day. Even though I don't care about that, it won't get me many votes. Maybe you could put some things in place for all the classes to get along. If somebody else wins, they're only gonna care about their own class. Please, Alec, why won't you do it for us?"

"Okay, sure, whatever," I said, just wanting them to leave me alone. However, that didn't keep me from hoping that someone else in our class might want to run.

Later, when we got back to our classroom, my plan was to get everybody to support someone else and this would all be over. It was a great idea and probably would have worked, until I saw Tyrod raise his hand to nominate himself. So when Morgan nominated me, I accepted—and it was on.

I had no other choice. There was no way I could let a guy who liked to make people feel small win class president. Even though the representative from our class had to run against people from the other three classrooms, I didn't want Tyrod to have a chance.

It was just the two of us running against each other. No speeches were necessary. Everyone wrote the name of their candidate of choice on slips of paper and passed them to our teacher. After twenty minutes, Dr. Richardson announced the winner. Tyrod jumped out of his chair when she said, "Alec London."

The class roared with cheers. But, of course, Tyrod made it known that he wasn't happy. My take was, if he wanted people to like him and vote for him, maybe next year in middle school he'd think about how he treats people. Too late for now, though, because I won!

● ● ●

"Pass those greens, that potato salad, and the yams," Grandma said, as she licked her lips. Looking at the delicious spread, who could blame her?

We were all smiling and happy. I was especially glad when Grandma came out of her room. It was good to see her so cheerful and acting like she had a ton of energy.

"Why y'all lookin' at me like I don't have nothin' to be thankful for? The Lord allowed me to see another Thanksgiving. I'm with my son, his beautiful wife, and my grand boys." Looking at Antoine and me, she smiled and said, "And, y'all aren't babies anymore." Grandma was beaming like the sun when she added, "Yes, thank the Lord . . . being with my family is like heaven on Earth. I feel fine!"

"Oh, Mom, we love you too," my mother said, as she got up from her seat to give Grandma a great big hug.

After they hugged for a second, Grandma held on to Mom's hand and said, "It's just good to have you home, Lisa. I've been tryin' to take good care of your men, but I can't do it like you. And me being a little sick and all hasn't helped. Now, pass the turkey, son."

"Antoine, how are your grades?" Dad asked, as he passed the platter to Grandma. He noticed how quickly Antoine was gobbling up his food so that he could be excused.

I know my brother. Whenever he tried to eat really fast, it was because he didn't want anyone to ask him any questions—particularly about school. Dad understood that fact too and gave Antoine a tough glare, as he waited for an answer.

"Mhhh umm. Ummm hum ummm hmmm," Antoine moaned with food stuffed in his mouth.

"Boy, you'd better hurry up and chew that food. Don't play with me. Your mother told me that she went on the I-Parent website and checked on your progress. Your grades are below average at best."

"Honey, we can talk about that later," Mom spoke up, as she leaned in closer to Dad.

"No, no, we can talk about this right now. You know your son is trying to avoid answering questions about school. Antoine's eating his food too fast; he's acting like he'll get a gold medal if he finishes before anyone else."

"Well, there's no need to ruin Thanksgiving dinner, talking about the tough stuff. Can we just enjoy each other for a while?"

"Yeah, you mean before you're gone again?" Dad blurted out.

"Oooohhhh! Please pass that cranberry sauce and those string beans," Grandma jumped in, picking up on the tension in the air between my parents.

Even Antoine noticed things were getting a little hot. So he tried to bring them back to his poor school performance. He figured that would be better than hearing our parents argue over their personal problems. With Mom being gone most of the time, there's been too much distance between my parents.

Antoine started, "Dad, I know I gotta work on my grades. Right now, they're not so good, but I've got exams comin' up and I'm gonna study real hard. Besides, I'm gonna do a really good job on a couple of papers that are due soon. My grades are gonna get better, Dad, you'll see."

At that point, our father wasn't showing any interest in what Antoine had to say. His attention was on Mom with a real serious look on his face. I don't know if she was using her acting skills or what. Mom kept eating her food slowly and coolly. You could almost see steam shooting out of Dad's ears, but she wasn't letting it get to her. She was ignoring him, and it was making him more furious.

"See, why are you going to do this? Why are you going to mess up a perfectly delightful dinner?" said Dad.

"Are you kidding? You're the one all hot under the collar, raising your voice and bringing up things that aren't pleasant. If anyone's ruining Thanksgiving, it's you. Don't blame me!"

"Now, just calm down, you two," Grandma said to my parents.

"No, he wants me home so badly. But when I'm here, this is what he does."

"Yeah, because you didn't come to stay! When are you leaving? You haven't even told us that."

Mom said, "Andre, you know I have to go back and shoot the last episode."

"No, you don't have to do that. That's a choice you're making. You used to have an excuse. We were behind in some bills. I wasn't working. Okay, there was more pressure on us then."

"Oh, and that's gone now?" Mom said sarcastically. "Maybe my coming home was a bad idea."

She got up from the table and put down her napkin. When she dashed away, Antoine looked at Dad like he had broken his heart. I didn't know how to feel, but I do agree with Dad. Mom was making a choice to be away from us by being an actress in Los Angeles. We needed her here.

However, after I visited her in California, I knew it was her dream. It just didn't seem right to ask her to give it up. I love them both, and I love my family being together. There had to be a way all this could work out. *"God, please help us,"* I prayed silently.

"May I be excused?" I asked, as I started to get up.

Dad said firmly, "No! Just sit down and finish eating. She's not going to ruin this Thanksgiving for us."

"Oh, let the boy go on and talk to his mama!" said Grandma.

Dad mumbled something and told me that I could leave. Having his permission, I got up from the table and went to knock on their bedroom door. While waiting for her to answer, I listened for a minute and could hear her crying.

"Mom, it's me. Alec. Please let me in. Please let me talk to you. Please open up. I care about you, Mom."

"Not right now, Alec. I don't . . . I don't want to talk right now. Okay? I'm sorry, baby."

It was really hard to accept that she was hurting so much. Even so, I couldn't blame Dad, because he was really going through a lot too. I could only imagine what he was thinking. He could lose both Grandma and his wife for good.

Thinking about the turkey and dressing on my plate, I went back to the dining room table. Everyone was looking at me like, "that was quick," so I said, "She wants to be alone."

"Urgh!" Dad grumbled, as he got up and left the table.

Mom told me that she wanted to be alone, but she was his wife. So Dad figured he should try and talk to her. Hopefully, they were going to work things out. Forgetting about the food in front of me, I held my head down and prayed, *"Lord, we need you."*

Sensing what I was doing, Grandma said, "Good! That's right, baby. Give it to the Lord."

"What good is that gonna do?" Antoine spoke up.

Grandma said, "Chile, God can fix it . . . and don't you forget it."

"Alec's been prayin' for God to fix it for a long time. Our parents still can't get along. Don't y'all see that? They hardly like each other, much less love each other."

"Oh, that's not true, Antoine," Grandma said. "You're makin' it sound worse than it really is. They do love each other, or they wouldn't be tryin' to work through all of this."

In her own way, Grandma then tried to explain something to us. "You boys are gettin' older now. I don't know how much longer I'm gonna be around, but one day I do know y'all are gonna be somebody's husbands . . . "

"Ewwwwww," Antoine said.

"That's right. Doesn't sound so good right now, does it? And, believe me, you should take your time. But like I was saying, one day I know you will . . . and your grand-daddy went on to be with the Lord when y'all were little. Ooooh, he was a good man! And there's one thing he always did right—he led the Lord's way."

"I don't understand, Grandma," I said.

"God wants the man to be the head of the household. That's why I'm lookin' at my son like he's done lost his marbles. There's a way to lead and there's a way to show your frustration. I just want you young men to know that if you put God first, even when you think there is no hope, God can work it out. So always remember that. Keep prayin', and keep believin'. Have faith in God, and take everything to Him in prayer. God will always help you. He can truly do anything but fail."

Our grandmother wasn't just saying empty words to us. She meant what she said, as tears fell from her eyes. We knew she loved us, but now it was plain to me that she loved God more. And she wanted us to have a strong relationship with God too. I don't really know what leading God's way means, but I was determined to find out some day.

One thing I did know. There was no need to worry about my parents. Their marriage was in God's hands—and I had no need to fear.

● ● ●

"Okay, so you've got your cupcakes, lollipops, flyers, and posters. You've practiced your speech and it sounds great. You're all set," Mom said, as she took inventory before dropping me off at school. It was Monday morning and the holiday break was over.

Pulling up to the walkway, she said, "That's a lot of stuff, Alec. Do you need me to help you carry it in?"

"No, Mom. I'm okay. "

Dad had gone to talk to Antoine's teachers, and I needed to be at school early. It was time to get ready for the election. Thankfully, Mom drove me, but I didn't want her to hang around.

Morgan, Trey, and Zarick all stuck by their word. They wore red T-shirts just like we agreed. I gave each of them a bunch of stuff. As kids came into the school, they were supposed to pass out the lollipops and flyers.

The cupcakes Mom baked were just for the fifth graders. I was hoping they would be an important part of helping me to win. At first, I didn't really want to do this. But now I'm kind of into it, and I definitely don't want to lose. It's just that knowing the fifth-grade class president is supposed to lead all the students was making me very nervous.

In fact, a lot was at stake. I wasn't doing this because someone else put me up to it anymore. Now I'm running because I have a purpose. We need unity in our school. Since my dad became the principal, he's done a lot to change things for the better. Kids are caring more about their grades. But there's always room for improvement. I believe a strong student leader could help make a difference. The scary thing about it is, if I lose, what would happen to my vision then?

Zarick came up to me and said, "We have to hang your posters."

"My posters are up," I said to him, wondering why he hadn't seen them.

"No, they're down on the floor. People are steppin' on them and everything."

I rushed down the hallway to see what he was talking about. Sure enough, my posters were lying in the middle of the floor. After we put them up again, I stood by the lockers and watched. Sure enough, Tyrod didn't see me, and he was about to take one down.

"What are you doin'?" I said to him.

"I'm just readin' your sign. Get out of my way."

He pushed me back.

"No, you're takin' my signs down."

"You don't have any proof of that. What you gonna do? Turn me in to your dad for nothin'? Get me all in trouble because you don't like me?"

Just then, I heard someone say, "Eww! Uhhh, yuck! There's an ant on my cupcake!" A girl screamed out, and Tyrod started laughing.

I went over to her, and she told me that Tyrod gave her one of my cupcakes.

"I'm not votin' for you, Alec London! You're tryin' to make people sick!"

I was headed back over to Tyrod to straighten him out, but Zarick held me back.

"No, no. Don't even waste your energy on him."

"Ants . . . on my cupcakes . . . really?" I was too upset.

"What?" Tyrod explained. "I just set the cupcake down . . . can't help it if a little ant crawled on it. I didn't want it, so I gave it to that girl. I told her to look out."

"Don't be mad because the class picked me to run. This is crazy. You're tryin' to sabotage my campaign," I told him.

"Whatever. You might've beat me, but you're not gonna win class president. I'm gonna see to that," Tyrod argued.

Zarick tugged me away. "Alec, ignore him. Just come on. Morgan is in our classroom. She wants to help you practice your speech one last time. And Trey already went to tell Dr. Richardson what's goin' on with Tyrod. No need to worry about him."

I just threw my hands up and hung my head low. This wasn't good. I felt beaten before the voting even started.

"Don't let Tyrod get to you!" Morgan said to me. "Zarick told me everything that's been goin' on. That boy's just jealous."

"It doesn't matter. I'm not cut out for this."

"Why are you sayin' that?"

"Because I wanted to punch him and that's not how leadership should act."

"But you didn't punch him."

"Yeah, only because Zarick held me back."

Morgan tried to convince me. "You've got good people around you who wanna see you succeed. We voted for you to be our leader. You can't back out now."

"Yes, I can."

"Okay, you're right. Yes, you can. But what purpose would that serve? We believe in you, Alec. You care about people, you're strong. Besides, deep down inside, I know you want this."

"How do you know that?"

"Well, you wouldn't be doin' it in the first place, if you didn't want to. Nobody can push you into anything. Alec, you have to pray about this, and do whatever God tells you to do. For real, forget what the rest of us want. I already know you can do it, but you've gotta know that for yourself."

After giving me good advice, she walked over to her desk. Still, I was having second thoughts because this was a lot. There were three other candidates, and I didn't know any of them. Maybe it was their time. Maybe one of them was supposed to be chosen to lead the class. Maybe it wasn't for me.

I sat down at my desk and continued to think it over. Then, a strange feeling started taking place inside me. Something was making me excited about this whole thing. Something was telling me that I was cut out to be the class president. Suddenly, I began to feel like I wasn't supposed to back out.

Immediately, I took Morgan's advice and prayed, *"Lord, right now, I'm a little frustrated and a little nervous, but I'm excited at the same time. Am I supposed to do this? If so, can You show me? Can You make it plain? Can You make it clear? Can You help me? In Jesus' name, I pray. Amen."*

When I finished praying, the thought of Mom helping me to make my posters came to mind. I remembered Dad listening to me going over my speech. I remembered Antoine helping me to pick out a fly outfit to wear. And I remembered Grandma giving me hugs and kisses, telling me I was going to be great. All that happened to give me confidence, to assure me that at least I needed to try. If I gave my all and did my best, then it wouldn't make a difference if I lost because I had done my part.

An hour later, when it was time for the four candidates to give our speeches, I confidently walked up to the podium and said, "Hi. I'm Alec London, ready to take the lead and be elected class president. We are the fifth-grade class, and together we can all learn to take the lead in life and in our education. I want to be class president because I care about all the students here—even the ones who need to understand that it's not cool to bully anybody. I care about the ones who are here for the right reason too. Those who are smart and getting As can take the lead in helping other students. And for those who are just trying to find your way, I want to help you."

I really felt like I was saying what the class needed to

hear. My stomach didn't feel so nervous anymore, and I kept on talking. "I had a speech. I practiced it and rehearsed it, but standing in front of you right now, I feel like I just need to speak from the heart. Yeah, you guys know that my dad is the principal of this school, but that has nothing to do with why I want to be class president. He's doing his part, and I want to do mine. If I'm elected, I won't let you down. At the end of the year, we're going to have a very cool fifth-grade carnival. On Field Day, we'll have it going on too. So, elect me, Alec London, and let me help you take the lead."

The crowd cheered with excitement. As the students dropped their ballots in the box, I had a good feeling. Then, at the end of the day, when Dad gave the afternoon announcements, he declared the winner. "Your next class president is—Alec London!"

My class was thrilled. Zarick gave me a high five. Trey started doing a dance, and Morgan hugged me. Seeing my friends acting so happy made me feel like a true winner!

Letter to Mom

Dear Mom,

Dr. Richardson announced that we had to choose a nominee from our class to run for 5th grade class president. My friends kept telling me I should run. At first I wasn't for it, but then I realized I might like the job.

I am so happy you were here to help me get my campaign materials together. I want to make you and Dad proud. I was a little nervous about the speech, but once I prayed, God helped me to deliver it.

Mom, your son won the election! Today, 5th grade class president. Tomorrow, president of the United States of America!

Your son,
Hopeful Alec

Word Search:
Track and Field Terms

Study the terms below that are often used at any track meet.

```
K  N  F  G  F  M  O  F  S  N  F  N
P  O  F  D  Q  Y  F  T  O  A  S  B
B  L  T  B  E  J  J  L  N  S  H  P
I  H  Z  K  J  C  H  P  J  M  O  G
F  T  I  W  Q  T  A  A  R  I  T  Z
D  A  Y  P  A  H  V  T  L  Q  P  W
S  T  W  T  S  E  S  T  H  T  U  X
U  N  P  O  L  E  V  A  U  L  T  C
M  E  Z  I  C  X  I  U  T  Z  O  B
H  P  N  S  C  S  I  D  B  C  V  N
E  U  R  A  D  S  V  V  B  D  J  E
H  T  N  S  Y  F  C  G  Q  K  B  K
```

DECATHLON	DISCS	HEPTATHLON
JAVELIN	PENTATHLON	POLE VAULT
SHOT PUT		

Personal
Pride

2

"Son, I'm really proud of you," my dad said to me, as he drove me to school. He had just announced the day before that I was voted class president.

"First of all, to get your class to vote for you as their representative was a big deal. Then you ran a good campaign and gave a great speech. I heard about some of the stuff that was going on with that young man Tyrod. Dr. Richardson took care of that and put him in his place. But Alec, I'm so glad you took the high road. You are a difference-maker, and you took the lead. People support you. I know you won't let them down."

I was waiting for Dad to say something else. He was setting me up too high to keep me there. Also, the way he was dragging it out, I knew there was more he wanted to tell me.

Finally, he said it. "BUT just make sure you don't get the big head. Remember, the qualities that got you elected are attributes that you need to keep. You understand?"

"Yes, sir," I said, looking away, a little dejected.

A part of me was wondering if he really was proud of me, or if he said all that just so he could add that last part. I sighed. I didn't want to let anyone down. Maybe I wasn't the right person for the job after all.

Picking up that something was wrong, Dad touched my shoulder and said, "Son, really, this is awesome. It's a very impressive accomplishment—better than ten touchdowns in my book. You did something amazing here, and I'm not trying to take anything away from that. I'm your dad, and I always want to tell you things to help keep you on the right track. Son, always do what's right."

I heard him and wanted to say, *Yeah, but Dad, you talk about doing what's right, and you're going around the house being extra tough and yelling all the time. You can't even see how you're pushing us away because of that.*

Instead, I didn't say anything because I didn't want him to get mad at me. When we pulled up to the school, it was time for me to do safety patrol duty. So we shook hands and went our separate ways.

"There he is, class president!" Trey called out when he saw me. He sounded like I was some kind of a star.

"Please stop. I'm the same old Alec," I said to him. In the back of my mind, I remembered my dad's words he just spoke to me about getting the big head. At the same time, I didn't want other people to inflate my head either.

I wasn't about to change, and I certainly didn't want

my friends to change around me. When Zarick stood in front of me and started bowing, it really started to irritate me.

Feeling uneasy, I said, "Okay, so what's up with all of that? Why you gotta go there? Being class president isn't that big a deal. It's just me. I'm just class president. Please calm down, or you're gonna make me quit already."

"I'm just teasin' you, man," Zarick said, placing his hand on my shoulder.

Trey took it a little personal when Zarick came up and cut into our conversation. He jumped in and told Zarick, "Yeah. Alec was sensitive like that with me too, but I was standin' here talkin' to him. Didn't you see that?"

Zarick didn't back away. "What? I can't talk to my friend?"

Trey stepped to Zarick and said, "Your friend? He's my friend!"

"Okay, okay, guys . . . " I said, getting in between the two of them. "I'm friends with you both. What's the big deal?"

"Fine, just be his friend then," Trey shot back at me and stormed away.

Then Zarick teased me, "I didn't mean to get you in trouble with your girlfriend."

"Okay, see . . . why you got jokes?" I asked him, shaking my head.

"Because he's such a wimp. Man, I don't even know why you like hangin' out with Trey anyway. He whines all

31

the time. He's not tough like us."

"I'm not tough like you and Tyrod," I said, a little defensive that he was getting on Trey.

"Oh, so why you gotta throw me in the same category as Tyrod . . . what you tryna say? You'd rather be a baby than a man?"

"Okay, who's the man?" I said to Zarick.

"Forget it."

"No, no, no, no, no," I said, before he walked away. "If we're gonna be friends, we have to be able to talk about what we both feel. You can't get sensitive and neither can I. You talkin' about Trey bein' a wimp? As soon as I come at you with how I feel, you wanna walk away. Wassup? Don't take it personal, I'm just tellin' you how I feel. Trey's my boy, and I don't like you pickin' on him or sayin' bad stuff about him. At the same time, you'd best believe I'm not gonna let him say anything about you. It's just how I roll. So don't walk away."

Zarick turned around and nodded. Then he said, "Cool. That's wassup. I hear you, and I respect that."

"Cool, then. I've gotta go, or I'll be late for my safety post. See ya in class," I said to my friend.

Fifteen minutes later, when the final bell rang for class to begin, it was time for us to go to P.E. We had physical education class once a week, and Coach Braxton was tough, but very cool. Everyone liked him.

The coach told the class, "Today, young people, we're doing the forty-yard dash. I'm looking for the best times.

Remember, you have to stay behind the line until I blow the whistle. Then, when it's time to go, I want you to keep accelerating until you cross the finish line down there," he explained, pointing at the other end of the gym. "Any questions?"

Trey raised his hand.

"Yes, Trey?"

"If we mess up . . . " Trey said, scratching his head, " . . . do we get to do it over?"

Coach Braxton replied, "Yes, I will allow you to do it over. Now, if it's excessive, then I'm not going to let you keep doing it over. I think we can all listen for the whistle and get it right the first time. But don't stress if you need to redo. I've got you."

"Thanks, Coach," said Trey.

Tyrod jumped on the line first and nobody wanted to stand beside him. If there was one class Tyrod excelled in, it was P.E. I found that out last summer when we were on the baseball team together. The boy was an outstanding athlete.

"Come on, Zarick, get right here," Coach Braxton called out, pointing to the spot next to Tyrod.

Zarick didn't want to, but he obeyed. Tyrod was smiling from Georgia to Florida, and that's a long way apart. As soon as Coach blew the whistle, Tyrod had Zarick eating his dust.

"Whew, Tyrod! Four-nine. Zarick, five-nine."

Coach Braxton called on some other people. Then, at

last, it was my turn. Standing with Trey, we waited for the whistle to blow. Trey leaned over and said, "Don't make me look bad."

"I'm just runnin', what are you talkin' about?"

I hadn't been timed in the forty, so I didn't know what I could do. When my time read four-nine, everybody started oooing and aaahing. Tyrod wanted a match.

"Oh, you saw how I made Zarick look bad. I'm really gonna turn the heat up now," he said to me.

Coach Braxton and the rest of the class were waiting down by the finish line. "All right, you guys, listen up! On your mark, get set . . . "

When he said go, something inside of me just kicked into another gear. I took off and didn't look to the side to see what Tyrod was doing. I just got fired up and felt like that little bird, the Road Runner. I was gone.

"Wow, that's a four-eight."

Tyrod was right behind me with another four-nine. He wasn't pleased and complained to Coach. "I didn't hear you say go. He took off before he was supposed to . . . "

Tyrod was making all kinds of excuses, but Coach Braxton wasn't hearing it. It didn't matter to me that he was upset, because it really felt good that I'd done my ultimate best. The icing on the cake was that I got a super time!

● ● ●

Back in the classroom, Tyrod came over to me and said, "Next time, I'm gonna beat you."

Oh, so now I'm supposed to be scared of him. Stepping in his face, I said, "Please. Any day, any time."

Dr. Richardson saw us arguing and before the class could crowd around, she said, "All right, everybody sit down! We have some serious work to start preparing for. Today, I want to talk to you about literary terms. Take out your notebooks and let's write down some words and definitions. The first word is, allegory, a-l-l-e-g-o-r-y. Definition: an extended metaphor in which objects, persons, and actions in a narrative are compared with a meaning that lies outside of the narrative."

We all looked at Dr. Richardson like she was speaking Spanish, Chinese, Japanese, and Vietnamese all at the same time. The definition of an allegory was something we didn't understand, and it went way over our heads.

She got that and said, "Okay, an allegory is a story with two meanings. It has a literal meaning and a symbolic meaning. For example, we could make up a story with Alec London as the main character, maybe a superhero. It could be a fable or a tale that takes place in historical times, like way back in the thirteen hundreds during the Middle English period when the superheroes of today didn't exist. We won't deal a lot with allegories. For now, you just need to know something about what they are."

Whew! It seemed like the sound of relief came from everyone in the room.

"The next word is ballad, b-a-l-l-a-d. A ballad is a narrative composition in rhythmic verse that tells a story. Basically, that means a written story that is put to song."

Morgan raised her hand.

"Yes, Morgan?"

"My mother loves ballads, especially the ones by this guy named Luther Vandross."

Dr. Richardson said, "Yes, so do I. Okay, moving on. The next word is drama, d-r-a-m-a. It is a composition made up in verse or prose that tells a story using dialogue and involves conflicts and emotions. A drama is intended to be acted out in a theatrical performance. Basically, it's a made-up story acted out by characters."

For a second, my mind wandered. That definition made me think of the drama that is sometimes a part of my life, and I wondered if I could write a play about it.

"Next, an epic, e-p-i-c, is a long, poetic narrative that usually has a hero as the main character. It is a work of art composed with a series of great achievements that highlight the character's heroic acts."

Tyrod raised his hand.

"Yes, Tyrod?"

"So, is Superman an epic?"

"Some consider it one, but epics are more of a historical nature. Think of stories about the Greek god Zeus, or the movie *Clash of the Titans*."

Tyrod looked like he was a little confused. He'd probably seen the movie, but I think he wanted to ask a question about the Greek god our teacher mentioned.

"Lastly, an ode, o-d-e, is a lyrical poem that typically creates an expressive feeling or enthusiastic emotion. An ode is a more serious type of poem. So right now I want you all to take some time and just be creative. Don't think too hard about it and write a ballad or an ode."

Zarick asked, "Do we have to rhyme?"

"Yes."

Dr. Richardson said, "You have forty minutes."

"Do we have to read them out loud in class?" I asked.

"I want you to write as if you would have to read them in front of the class." Hearing some sounds from the class that she didn't like, our teacher said, "Young people, I don't need you to complain, I need you to buckle down and get this. It's time to expand your writing skills and take it up to the next level. We haven't even talked about fables and satires, or rhymes, limericks, and sonnets yet. We're going to get there, but right now I want you to take this exercise seriously. So get to work. If you need to, raise your hand, and I'll come around to you individually."

After ten minutes of looking at my blank paper, words just started to flow. I wrote a ballad to my mom, telling her how much I love her and miss her when she's gone.

When I turned in my paper, Dr. Richardson handed me a note. I couldn't wait to get back to my desk and open it. It was from Coach Braxton and read:

Dear Alec,

You did a really good job today. I talked to your dad, and he said that I can speak to you after school. Please come directly to my office in the gym. Thanks.

Coach Braxton

I wondered what he wanted to talk to me about. So many questions were running through my mind. Did he want to retest me? Did he believe that I started too early after all? Was my foot over the line and that means my four-eight time in the forty is invalid? Maybe his watch was broken and he wanted to do it over for that reason. Or maybe, just maybe, there were other people that he wanted me to run against. And if that was the case, could I do it again? I had to admit, the thought of beating Tyrod and hushing him up definitely made me excited.

When I got down to his office, the coach wasn't there and his door was locked. Just as I was about to sit down by the door, I heard an annoying voice.

"Why are you here?"

I turned around, and it was Tyrod.

"Why are you here?" I asked him back. I didn't need to give him any explanation.

Then he held out a note. It was just like the one Coach Braxton sent me. At first, I thought maybe I'd dropped mine and he had it. But Tyrod's name was at the top of his. I reached in my book bag, pulled out my note, and showed it to him.

"He asked you to come too?" I was stunned.

Being difficult as usual, Tyrod said, "That's what the note says, doesn't it?"

I didn't want to get smart with Tyrod, so I gritted my teeth and looked away. He always got on my nerves, trying to act like he knows everything. Even though I didn't know why Coach Braxton wanted to see me, I definitely didn't want to be here with Tyrod. I didn't want to race him again. I didn't want to be around him.

Picking up my book bag, I was getting ready to leave when Coach Braxton walked in. "All right, boys, settle down. I could hear you halfway down the hall."

When he unlocked his office door, Tyrod and I didn't move. Coach gave us a tough look, and the three of us went inside.

Coach didn't waste any time. He started, "Sit down, boys. It's ridiculous for the both of you to be so talented, so athletically gifted, and you don't even realize the power of what teamwork could do with such skills."

"We've been on the same team before, sir," I said quickly.

"Yeah, and ummm, I tried to teach him lessons back then," Tyrod said, like I ever needed his help. "He still doesn't appreciate my skills."

"Whatever," I said under my breath.

"Well, I don't know what you all did before, or what coach you had. I can tell you that I'm coaching an elite track team, and I want both of you young men to be on it.

I've talked to your parents and they're for it. So really, you don't get a choice—"

After that, he didn't say anything more. He just stopped mid-sentence and looked at us. What did he expect me to say? If I really didn't have a choice in whether I'd run track, then I had no response. Tyrod was quiet too.

"I'm just kidding, you always have a choice. Your parents do want you to participate because track and field is another one of those sports that could lead to a great scholarship one day. And since you guys are only in the fifth grade running a forty under five seconds, I need to be working with you both. Can you put aside your differences so we can take your game up to a whole new level? I care about both of you young men. I think if I work with the two of you, I can help build your character," Coach said, as he looked at me.

Then, looking right at Tyrod, he finished with, "And instill even better attributes in you. So what do you say?"

Personally, I didn't know what to say. I looked at Tyrod and, with a nod, we both said, "Okay."

● ● ●

At long last, it was Christmas morning. To my surprise and joy, I got everything a young boy could want. New kicks, the latest clothes, updated video games, a bigger bicycle, and money.

Well, I guess I got everything I wanted, except for one thing—a peaceful household. My parents were locked in their room, arguing. I guess they thought Antoine, Grandma, and I couldn't hear them. Although I couldn't make out every word, it's pretty clear they were having trouble sharing the same space. How much longer could this go on? I opened up my door when I heard my grandmother standing at their door.

"Open up! Open up this door, let me in here!"

Dad came out and said, "Mom, we're talking."

"I understand that. You've gotta understand that the boys and I can hear everything. Now you two are grown, and I can't tell you what to do. But I'm old, and I'm gonna speak my mind anyway because I love you all. This is Christmas day. It's the day that we're supposed to celebrate the fact that God sent His only Son to be born into this world to save us all. And I'm not gonna spend this special day havin' my heart racin' because y'all are makin' me feel uncomfortable!"

"All right, Mom, all right."

"No, no, no, it's not all right and I'm not finished. Y'all givin' these boys a whole bunch of stuff, and they don't need no more stuff. They need their parents sittin' down with them, spendin' some time with them. That's what wrong with parents nowadays. You give these kids everything, but you don't give them yourselves."

Antoine opened his door wide and shouted, "I don't need them talkin' to me."

"Oh hush, boy. Yes, you do. You sittin' around here moping worse than your little brother."

"I'm so sorry. I didn't realize we were that loud," Mom said, as she came out of the room.

"Well, you were that loud, honey," Grandma told her gently.

At that moment, the five of us were standing in the hallway of our home. We were looking at each other, not knowing what else to say. So I just began to silently pray, *"Lord, I know it's hard for parents to make ends meet, to handle all the big adult problems in the world and all of the stuff they've got to deal with. I used to think that I couldn't wait to be grown one day, but now I see I don't have it so bad as a kid. My life isn't perfect, but I don't have big people problems. And for that I'm thankful. I need You right now to help us. Help us get along, help us heal, help us just be a close family. Grandma is right, everything's not wonderful. But this is a special day, and we should only be focusing on what's good."*

"Antoine, Alec, I'm sorry. We'll try and do better. I promise. How about playing some games right now?" Mom asked, as my prayer ended.

Getting excited, I said, "Games, yeah, that'll be fun!"

"Games . . . " I heard Dad mumble, as he went back into their room.

Mom, Grandma, and Antoine headed to the kitchen table to play Monopoly.

I stepped into the room with Dad and said, "Can I speak to you for a second?"

He looked at me, sat down on the edge of the bed, and

put both his hands on his head. "Yes, son?"

"Is it okay if I really, really share with you from my heart? I don't want you to get mad at me or anything."

He took a deep breath and said, "Sure, talk."

"You're always tellin' me things that could help me be a better person. I know that's your job because you're my dad. And as your son, I want you to know I try and take in everything you tell me. I wanna be the best Alec I can be."

"What's on your mind, son? What do you want to share?"

"A couple of years ago when you were out of a job and going to school for your doctorate, do you remember how things were around here?"

"Well, it wasn't my finest hour. I will say that. Honestly, I felt like I'd let you guys down. Without having a job, I wasn't able to provide for you the way I'm supposed to . . . and there were bills to be paid. It was just a lot. I'm sorry for how I behaved."

"Well, I know, Dad. But the thing is, Mom cried a lot, and you were really a different, not-so-nice person. I was glad when that person finally left. But these past few weeks that person has been tryin' to come back. I know it's because you want Mom to stay home. I want her to stay too, but I just don't ever want you to be that mean person again."

Dad's eyes started to tear up. "I hear what you're saying, son. It takes a strong person to come and talk to me about these things. Your Mom and I do love each other. It may not seem like it, but we do. She's a strong lady when she makes up her mind."

I smiled. "You can say that again."

My dad said, "But I do know that God has called me to lead this family. In doing so, He humbles me because I'm not always right. So I'm going to do a better job of listening to your Mom and your Grandma and you boys too. I'm going to get this thing together. We're going to be okay."

He hugged me really tight. God made the difference. We played games and ate some of Grandma's good cooking. Besides, every game we played, I came in first place. Beating everyone in my family, especially Antoine, gave me some personal pride.

Letter to Mom

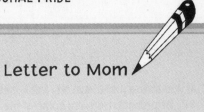

Dear Mom,

    I was amazing in P.E. I can run super fast. Tyrod used to be the fastest at our school, and now he's mad that I've taken that honor.

    Coach Braxton was so impressed with both of us that he's asked us to be on his elite track team. Mom, I'm not sure if I want that. Dad thinks it will be good though. I would ask you to talk to him for me, but, honestly, it's been tough hearing you two argue.

    I'm glad Grandma convinced you both to stop fussing. It's Christmastime and we should be happy. Are you happy, Mom? I know that I'm happy you're home.

                 Your son,
                 Satisfied Alec

Word Search:
Track and Field Items

If you attend just about any track meet, there are certain items that will be present. Here are some of the important items that you will find around the sport.

```
N  T  Y  U  Q  T  K  S  I  L  C  S
I  U  L  G  H  R  A  T  M  K  S  P
Q  L  G  C  V  W  I  F  P  R  H  I
H  U  R  D  L  E  X  B  E  K  K  K
X  C  S  C  F  E  U  M  B  B  H  E
T  N  L  A  D  E  M  H  A  O  M  S
I  S  F  G  J  A  L  T  J  V  N  S
O  D  R  F  H  H  O  L  L  D  A  C
H  K  Y  H  F  N  J  E  J  U  O  F
T  D  W  J  L  E  Z  P  E  Y  A  R
N  K  K  M  S  K  Y  M  Z  V  I  U
A  P  S  Y  X  C  P  M  V  J  Y  L
```

BATON	GUN	HAMMERS
HURDLE	MEDAL	RIBBON	SPIKES

Tough Spot

3

"But Mom, I just can't invite one person over to spend the night on New Year's Eve. I've got two friends and they're both in my class. If one finds out that the other came and he wasn't invited, it's not gonna be good for me. You're the one who encouraged me to be Zarick's friend. So I can't leave him out. And Trey always invites me to hang out with him and his family. So I can't leave him out."

I was making a good case for her to give in. "Please, Mom. Please let me have two friends over," I begged.

"All right, Alec. But I don't want to hear a lot of noise. Besides, I guess it won't be so bad since Antoine is going to hang out at his friend's house."

I wanted to say, *Do you know exactly who Antoine's gonna be hangin' out with and what they're gonna to be doin'?* But I left that alone. Antoine is as slick as they come. I heard him on the phone planning something secretive with his buddy.

Because I wanted to consider my two friends' feelings, I needed to tell Zarick that Trey was coming. And I had to tell Trey that Zarick was coming. It didn't seem right to surprise either one of them. I also got the benefit of inviting both of my buddies. That way, if either one didn't want to come, or couldn't come, I would still have somebody to hang out with.

My grandma was going to be with her sister, and my parents were going to be downstairs with some of their friends. So if Trey and Zarick both said no, I'd be alone. Actually, I guess that wouldn't be so bad because I could use the alone time to begin planning all of the things I wanted to do for the end of the school year activities.

"Why'd you have to invite him?" asked Trey. "You don't think I'm cool enough to be with, huh?"

I didn't know where that comment was coming from. Trey didn't need to start acting needy, clingy, and whiney. I mean, he is my boy. He should already know I think he's cool. We went to the Falcons' football game together. Besides, Trey proved that he's no pushover. There's no way I could forget when we were in the second grade, and I was acting more like Tyrod by pushing people around. Trey stood up to me and demanded I stop acting crazy. For that reason alone, I never underestimate him.

Besides, I know he cares about me. Knowing what it's like to have a friend go to bat for you like he's done for me, I wasn't going to mess that up. At least, I wouldn't do that on purpose. Sometimes my attitude gets in the way, and I just don't want to be around anybody, but I'm working on it. What more can I say?

Taking a deep breath, I said into the telephone receiver, "Look, Trey, I'm invitin' you to come over to my house. It's not a party. It's just gonna be me and a couple of my cool friends bringin' in the New Year together. If you're down to come, you're welcome. But everybody here is gonna to get along. So what do you want to do?"

His answer was quick. "Well, I wanna come! I'll ask my parents and call you back."

"Sounds good," I said, before hanging up and immediately calling Zarick.

"Hey, Alec, what's goin' on?"

"Nothin' too much . . . just checkin' to see, if you have plans for tonight."

"Nope, and it's just a little crowded where we're stayin'. What're you up to?"

"Well, my mom said I could have some company, so I was tryin' to see if you wanted to come over."

"That sounds cool with me. It'll be fun, me and you hangin' out. You know I'm gonna beat you in some video games, right?"

"Well, it's not just gonna be me and you," I told Zarick.

"I don't understand. Is your brother gonna be there? I'm okay with that. He's cool."

"No, my brother's gonna hang out with one of his friends. It's gonna be—"

Cutting me off, Zarick said, "No, no, no, no, I know you're not sayin' it's gonna be that Trey guy from our class. Nuh-uh, I'm not hangin' out with him."

"Zarick, I already invited him, and I'm askin' you to come too. Give him a chance. I think with all that Tyrod stuff goin' on, we all got off on the wrong track. But this is different. It'll be fun. Trust me!"

Four hours later, they arrived at almost the same time. After we'd been together for about thirty minutes, it wasn't fun. Trey and Zarick weren't talking to each other. When I asked them what they wanted to do first, one wanted to go outside, and the other wanted to play video games. When I offered them something to eat, one wanted hamburgers, and the other wanted hot dogs.

I was getting more frustrated by the minute. When I turned on the TV, one wanted to watch sporting events, and one wanted to watch a scary movie. My two friends didn't agree on anything. Grandma would say they were acting like oil and vinegar, not wanting to mix at all.

Finally, I said, "Look, if we're gonna have any kind of fun, we've gotta learn to get along. You guys are makin' this real uncomfortable for me. I invited both of you over, and both of you accepted knowin' the other was comin'. At least, you need to make an effort."

Still, the way they were looking at each other, I felt like it was useless to try and get them to work it out. The tension was so heavy. My two buddies bonding seemed like a lost cause.

Zarick vented. "I'm gonna have to move pretty soon, so you really shouldn't have even invited Trey to come."

Trey argued, "Well, I've been his boy for way longer than you. He shouldn't have invited you to come."

"Did y'all hear anything I said?" I voiced my frustration. "Why don't both of you just go home. I'd rather be here by myself for New Year's Eve. You two fightin' each other for no reason is just crazy."

They both looked at me. I was serious. But neither of them moved to call their moms.

"You guys aren't so different," I said to them when no one got up to leave. "You both like sports and you both like action movies, and so do I. Why can't we flip a coin or just pick which one we're gonna do first? We've got all night, so we can do it all. Besides, we all love hotdogs and hamburgers, and Mom cooked both. So we can take our pick. First, we can go outside and then play video games later. Now I'm gonna go and help my mom, and when I come back, the two of y'all better be talkin'. Or, for real, I'm kickin' y'all out."

When I went into the kitchen, Mom was all smiles. She pinched my cheeks. Then she kissed my forehead.

"You heard me, huh?" I asked.

"You're just such a smart boy, I love you, love you, love you . . ." she said, as the kisses continued.

With a wet face, I pulled back. "Mom!"

"I know you're growing up, Alec, and this is your last year in elementary school. But you're still my baby. I'm just so proud of you. You wanted both of your friends to come. And even though it's been difficult, you're being a big boy and getting them to work it out. You're learning how to be a leader, and I like that you bring out the best in people."

"Then what about you and Dad? I wish I could bring out the best in the two of you."

"You and your Dad talked, and he told you we're going to work things out. I don't want you worrying about us."

"But y'all are my parents!"

"And like I said, we've got this. I've got a feeling everything is cool with your friends now. So head on back in there and play for a little while. Dinner will be ready soon."

"We're gonna go outside. Is that okay?"

"Sure."

I'd been talking with my mom for only a few minutes. And when I went back to the family room, the two of them where laughing. They were giving each other a fist bump. I was amazed.

"You're right," Trey said, when he saw me at the door. "I've gotta learn to share you, and I guess it won't be so bad since he's movin' away." I was about to get mad when I saw the hurt look on Zarick's face. Then Trey let us know that he was joking. He waited a second on purpose and then said, "Naw, I'm just playin'."

Zarick spoke next. "He's not that bad either. You think he's cool, and since I've been talkin' to him, he really is. His dad is chaplain of the Falcons, and I'm about to have

Trey kick you to the curb so I can go to the next game with him," he said with a grin.

I just laughed because, if that's what it would take for them to bond, it'd be cool with me. I couldn't hold my friends so close that they'd only hang out with me. If we were all going to be boys, then I had to step back and let them be friends too.

All of this reminded me of how upset I was when Morgan and Zarick became friends. That didn't feel good, and I didn't want it to happen again. Yeah, it looks like I'm growing up and learning what leadership is all about. In a whole lot of ways, it's not easy. But the three of us hanging out and having a good time was worth it.

● ● ●

Ever since my grandmother had a talk with my parents, we've really been getting along great as a family. Although I didn't want to think about it, in a couple days Mom would be headed back to California to tape another episode of her show.

However, there was no need to focus on that when we were having such a good time. In addition to Mom leaving in a couple days, school was about to start back. The time out had been great for the whole family.

Sitting in my room, I was having some quiet time and thinking about everything. Feeling pretty good about stuff, this seemed like a good time to turn my focus back to doing my best in school. My fifth-grade year started out a little rough with me getting some Cs and not trying as hard as I needed to. Now, I was determined to give it my all. When we returned, Dr. Richardson said we would have a test on literary terms. It was time to study and get serious; I had to be prepared.

Before the holiday break, we were focused on story comprehension. I learned that the *setting* is where a story takes place. The *theme* is the overall message of the story. The *plot* is what happens in the beginning, middle, and end. The *conflict* is the problem that needs to be solved. The *protagonist* is the good character. The *antagonist* is the bad character.

On top of all that, *characterization* refers to things about the characters that you understand from reading the story. For example, was a character mean, nice, scared, adventurous, or stuff like that. *Point of view* tells whether the story is told from first person, meaning the main character told it from their point of view. In that case, the writer uses the pronoun "I." If a story is written in third person, a narrator is telling the story.

This was great, I was studying, and it was paying off. Suddenly, there was a knock on my door. I looked up and saw my father standing there. I didn't know how long he'd been watching me, but the way he was looking at me seemed like he was proud.

"Come on in, Dad," I said. "I'm done, unless you want to quiz me. I know this stuff."

"I'm proud of you, son. I've been saying that, and you

are really coming around. But I want to talk to you about something."

"Yes, sir?" I said, placing my notebook down.

"Morgan's grandfather called me."

"Really?" I asked, as my eyes started squinting. I was wondering what that conversation was about.

"A couple of years ago, you went with his family to a car show and dinner or something. Right?"

"Yes, sir."

"Did you have fun? Did you like it?"

"Yeah, we had a good time. Her granddad is really cool."

"Well, he thinks highly of you too. He and his wife are taking Morgan to see the play *The Wiz*. They wanted to know if you could go. Afterward, they're going out to dinner. What do you think of that?"

"Yeah, I'd love to go!" I said, as my eyes got really wide.

"I thought you would."

"It's okay, right? I'll be in good hands with them."

"Yeah, but a couple of years ago Morgan was your friend. Now you're giving her flowers and she makes your heart go pitter-patter. I'm just not sure if this is a good idea."

"Dad!"

"You're young, son. Girls have their proper place . . . and I just . . . I don't know. I have to protect my boy. That's all I'm concerned about."

"Dad!" I said again.

"Why should I let you go?" he asked me.

"Because Morgan is my good friend, and her grandparents are inviting me. You always say I need to do things I haven't done, and going to a play seems like it would be real cool. I've only seen the movie *The Wiz* on TV, with Michael Jackson starring in it. I'd love to experience the story in a different way. I'm not going to do anything wrong. I know she's not my girlfriend. When is it?"

"Tommorow. I'll talk to your mom, and we'll see."

On the day of my outing, over dinner, breakfast, and lunch, every member of my family teased me. Even though it definitely wasn't a date, I was nervous. After the first hurdle was out of the way, and my parents were going to let me go, I had to figure out what to wear. Since nothing I pulled out of my closet seemed just right, Mom was kind enough to take me to the mall so we could go shopping.

"I didn't get Morgan a Christmas present, Mom, can I get her something now?"

"Oh, my young man is just so precious," she said, as she turned to me and pinched my cheeks.

I knew Mom was going to be leaving soon, but she was over-the-top emotional. She took me to a store called Things to Remember where I was able to get Morgan an engraved jewelry box.

Later that afternoon, I was really excited to be in the theater. When the lights were dimmed and the curtains were raised, I was so ready to see the acts. We'd been studying play formats in school, and it was easy for me to follow along. The actors were outstanding in this version of the familiar story. I really enjoyed the music and the whole play experience.

Next, we went to dinner. I was so nervous that it felt like worms were squirming around in my stomach. When I had to talk, I dropped my fork. I forgot that my mom told me to place my napkin in my lap. I didn't know which drink was mine. The whole thing was awkward, and everything seemed to be going wrong.

Her grandfather saw that I was uneasy. So when Morgan and her grandmother went to the restroom, he said, "Son, let me tell you something. I just think you're a wonderful young man. Relax. Don't hold back. There's no need to be restless, just spit out what you're trying to say."

"I just don't know how to act around a girl, sir. My brother, Antoine, is in the seventh grade. He told me that I shouldn't be too sweet because girls like boys to be mean. But then my mom says I should be really nice because girls like that. And my dad says I'm too young to like anybody. I know you're Morgan's granddad, so I really don't know why I'm tellin' you all this, but it just feels weird when I'm around her. A while ago, I got real jealous when somebody else at school liked her. One time, I hurt her feelings because things going on in my life were upsetting me. I didn't like that at all. In fact, I don't like the way I'm feeling now. All that's pretty bad, huh? Are you gonna tell Morgan never to talk to me again?"

He just started laughing, and that made me confused. I

didn't want to be so honest, but it just came tumbling out. I wished I could take back every word I'd said, but that was impossible.

There I was feeling real uncomfortable, until he put his hand on my shoulder and said, "You're a good young lad. The one thing I've learned from helping to raise Morgan is that you young people have a lot to deal with. I wouldn't say you're growing up too fast, and I certainly don't want to make light of your feelings. The first girl I had a crush on is the one who just went to the ladies' room with my granddaughter."

"But, I don't wanna get married!" I said with my eyes wider than an open car door.

"Don't even think about it. If you try anything, you're going to get a knuckle sandwich," he said, as he playfully balled up his fist to me. "But, what I'm saying is, I know that Morgan is blessed to have a young man who thinks she's something special. Don't make so much of your feelings; just be a good friend to her. I'm sure she cares about you too. And as long as you treat her better than you'd want to be treated, you'll have no problems with me, her stepdad, or her dad who's in the Navy. You got it?" he said, as he firmly patted me on the back.

When Morgan came back to the table, she looked at me like, *I hope my granddad didn't say anything to embarrass me.* But her grandfather and I actually had a good man-to-man conversation. He helped me to understand that these mixed up feelings I was having for a girl weren't

58

so bad after all. The only thing I needed to do was focus on being Morgan's friend and not hurt her feelings anymore. After that, I was able to quit being uneasy and get through the rest of my dinner.

In the evening when I got home, I was smiling because I'd had a great time.

● ● ●

"Dad, it's too cold to be runnin'." It was early Saturday morning, and my father was taking me to my first track practice.

"It's called cross-country. Alec, people do this all the time, as long as there's no snow on the ground. And we're in Georgia, so you're not going to see much of that. You'll be fine. You just need to toughen up some," Dad said, as he grabbed me by my shoulders in a tight squeeze.

I wanted to say, *I am tough, I didn't cry when Mom left to go back to California like you did.* But of course I wouldn't say anything disrespectful to my father.

Besides, I knew Dad didn't want to hear me complain. He would only give me the same old speech he gave when he took me to baseball camp last summer. I didn't want to go then either. That's when he told me, "Try something new, expand your horizons, you'll never know until you give it a whirl." Well, I wasn't trying to learn how to play baseball or dance then, and I certainly didn't want to run in the cold now.

"Son, you need to keep busy."

"Okay, but this is basketball season, Dad. I want to be busy playin' that."

"You've been playing basketball long enough; it's time for something new. And you're the one who gave the coach your word that you'd do this."

"Yes, sir," I said, regretting I'd ever agreed.

However, my attitude changed when we pulled up to the gym. I was impressed to see so many high schools boys who were ripped! I didn't know if they played football or if they wrestled or what. But they were cut and they were out there—ready to run. It was awesome, and now my mind was open to this. Because, if they could look like that running track, then this could only help improve my skinny, little body.

"What's up, home skillet? I'm Deuce," this real cool boy with dreads said to me. His muscles were so tight, they almost looked fake. He saw me staring and said, "Oh, that's hard work! I hear you've got skills. Coach wants me to work with you. Ready to stretch?"

"Stretch? Can't we just run?"

"No, you've gotta warm up first, or you might pull somethin'." He started bending and stretching his long legs.

"Is Deuce your real name?"

"Naw, but I'm not gonna tell you what it is, so just call me Deuce."

"Okay," I said.

"And you're Alec London. Do you have a nickname?"

"No, people just call me Alec."

"All right, all right, what events in track do you think you wanna run?"

"Forty-yard dash," I said, imagining myself flying.

"What else?"

Realizing I didn't know much about the sport, I asked, "Is there somethin' else?"

"Yep, it's a whole lot of things: the hurdles, the hundred meters, the relay race, the broad jump, standing jump, the mile. Don't you watch the Olympics?"

I shook my head no. "Football twenty-four seven is just fine for me . . . sometimes basketball . . . but definitely in the summertime during NBA playoff time. To me, track and field was always foreign," I told him.

"Well, if you're good at football or basketball, bein' in track can only enhance your skills in those sports too."

"You play other sports?" I asked Deuce.

"Yeah, I'm a runnin' back at the local high school here in DeKalb."

Just then, Coach Braxton heard our conversation and added, "And a highly recruited Division 1 football player. He'll be going to Georgia or Georgia Tech next."

"Cool," I said, as I turned my head and noticed Tyrod standing with another high school athlete. He was looking over and pointing at me.

"That's the other guy from your class, right?" Deuce asked when he saw me frowning.

"I guess."

"Oh, y'all have a beef?"

"You can tell?" I said, under my breath.

"Man, y'all are teammates. Y'all gotta squash all that."

"Whatever. He doesn't like me, and we've never been able to get along. I can't even pretend to like him."

"Is he the first person you've ever had a problem with?"

"No."

"How about the other people? Do y'all get along now?"

Flaring my nostrils, wanting Deuce to understand, I said, "Tyrod is different."

"I'm just askin'. Do you and anybody else you had a beef with get along?"

"Yeah, actually they're my boys now."

"Well, how did that all come about? Because you strike me as a leader; you know, somebody who squashes all the drama. You seem like someone who takes charge and settles stuff. You know about bein' the bigger man and all that, right?"

"Yeah, that happened okay in other situations, but this guy . . . you just have to know him . . . "

Deuce cut me off and said, "Coach brags on you and says you've got skills. I've been workin' with him since I was in elementary school. Now I'm excited that I have lots of opportunities to play D-1 ball. My parents can't afford to send me to college, so gettin' a scholarship is gonna be a major thing. But it's more than just academics and athletics, nowadays it's also about character."

"I don't understand."

"Well, a lot of people are messin' themselves up and not gettin' golden opportunities to go to college because they're doin' the wrong things. You know, can't get along with people and makin' dumb decisions. But it's good to be the bigger person and continue to practice excellence," Deuce said, as I nodded.

Coach Braxton called out, "All right guys, gather round. I want to introduce you to my dear friend, Derrick Moore. Derrick played in the NFL for a number of years and speaks to teams across the country. Give him a warm welcome."

As we clapped for him, the confident man looked us square in the eyes and said, "Well, I just came over today to introduce myself to you guys. I'm Coach Derrick Moore, and I'm excited to be with you guys. I know you're ready to win, and I'm going to be doing a series of sessions with you. First, I want to drop this nugget. We're going to look at our time together and this season as a journey. At the end of the season, you're going to be champions standing on the mountaintop. My program will help you get there. It's called C.L.I.M.B., which stands for Championship Leadership Is My Behavior."

Coach Moore sounded like a serious man who wanted to inspire young people. I could tell he wasn't trying to sugarcoat this stuff when he said, "You've got to work for it. You've got to want it. You've got to be willing. Because this is a team sport, we've all got to get there together. Do I have any champions here? I want to be clear with you, climbing the mountain isn't going to be easy. You'll be challenged and want to quit, but I'm not going to let you stay down and be in any tough spot."

Letter to Mom

Dear Mom,

Thank you for letting me invite Zarick and Trey over. It wasn't easy making sure they got along, but thanks to you teaching me how to care about others more than I care about myself, I was able to get them to give each other a try.

Also, thanks to you, I looked really good when I went with Morgan to the play. The outfit you got me was great. I think I like her, Mom, but it seems weird. Her grandfather was really cool about it. He told me to just keep being her friend and don't think about all the other stuff. Don't worry, she's not my girlfriend or anything like that, but I do care about her.

I went to track practice with Dad today and it's going to be harder than I thought. Help!

Your son,
Changing Alec

Word Search:
Track and Field Items

In the sport of track and field, there are several events. Some events are running, some are jumping, and some are combined. Listed below are some of these events.

```
F  G  U  H  C  J  K  Y  R  G  D  C
B  B  W  F  J  D  Z  C  J  S  R  D
O  N  U  K  K  I  O  S  S  P  X  U
D  I  S  T  A  N  C  E  P  M  Q  M
C  X  C  W  L  E  U  H  R  U  G  Y
S  O  A  Y  F  B  U  X  I  J  R  Y
N  Y  M  W  X  R  D  M  N  O  L  A
P  Y  A  B  D  D  N  O  T  D  O  O
Q  L  P  L  I  C  N  Q  S  N  S  P
T  J  E  C  E  N  S  W  O  R  H  T
H  S  Q  F  H  R  E  P  E  F  N  F
B  M  E  I  E  G  X  D  K  S  P  A
```

COMBINED   DISTANCE   HURDLES

JUMPS   RELAYS   SPRINTS   THROWS

Feel Better

4

"**Okay, Alec, I** know I'm not always the best brother. I know sometimes I might say things that sound mean. I might take the remote away from you, and I might get you in trouble. But you know deep down you're my boy. Right?"

Antoine was up to something when he came into my room with his book bag and a slight grin.

I didn't have to say, "What do you want?" because my face showed that expression. We hadn't been fussing lately, but he was definitely trying to butter me up. Then he just started twiddling his thumbs like he wanted to say something to me, but couldn't find the right words.

So I went back to studying. Antoine could stand there all day, but I was working. Finally, when he saw that he was being ignored, he found the courage to speak.

"Okay, it's like this," he said. "I need your help. You know I'm not really doin' good in school, right?"

I really didn't know what my brother's grades were. I

just knew Dad had been on him pretty hard about it. I had my own grades to pull up, so that's where my focus has been.

"School is hard for me, Alec, and middle school is really tough."

I wanted to tell him, *You didn't do well in elementary school either*, but I didn't want to go there and make him feel bad. I just nodded. We'd already been through this before. I told him anytime he wanted me to help him study I was willing.

It seemed like he was dragging out what he wanted to ask me, so I said, "I might not know how to do it, but we can find the directions in your book. What do you need help with? You're really smart, Antoine, if you'd just try harder."

However, he wasn't taking off his book bag. He wasn't opening up for me to figure out what was going on. Tired of trying to read his mind, I threw my hands up and waited for him to explain.

After a couple of minutes, Antoine said, "Okay, it's not in the book like that. I don't need you to help me read the directions. I need something bigger than that."

"What? I've got to read it to figure out how to teach it to you. If we read it together, maybe it would click what the teacher's been sayin'."

Antoine shook his head. "This isn't like social studies, science, or math. This is English."

"They have the definitions and directions in the

English books too, Antoine."

"See, you're not feelin' what I'm sayin'. My problem is, I have to write a paper."

"Oh, okay. That's easy."

"See, Alec, it's easy for you. It's not easy for me."

"Well, if you write the paper, I can proofread it. Or, I can help you outline it to get you started. Dr. Richardson told us to just write. Don't even think about it. You can always correct it and make it better later."

Antoine huffed, "I tried that. Go look in my room. My trash can is full of balled-up pieces of paper that I messed up. I can't write. I don't know how to do it."

"Mom and Dad said we're not supposed to say the word can't."

"So what! I'm sayin' can't. Okay? Are you gonna help me or not?" Antoine shouted with a bit of an attitude.

"Okay, what do you want me to do?" I was getting equally loud and frustrated with my brother. Antoine wasn't explaining enough for me to know what he needed from me.

Coming closer and talking more kindly, he said, "If you really wanna help me and not let me fail the seventh grade, I need you to write the paper for me."

My head did a double take. I know he didn't say what I thought he just said. Me? Write the paper for him? Now he was really trippin'.

"No!" I quickly replied.

"I don't need you to say no. Didn't you just hear me

ask you really, really nicely? I'm almost beggin' you not to leave me out here, because this paper can make or break my semester. It's got to be right. I've got an F in this class right now. I need an A paper and I don't never ask you for nothin'. Don't just leave me hangin'. Just write somethin' real quick and help me out. Please, Alec."

"But what if Dad finds out?"

"Nobody's gonna know if you keep your mouth shut. I'm gonna take the paper you write and type it up. So it's not gonna matter because the final paper won't even be in your handwriting."

Antoine's eyes were starting to tear up, like he'd been cutting an onion or something. When he turned around to head out, it seemed like he really did need me.

"Wait." I got in front of him, sighed, and said, "Okay, I'll do it."

"Thank you, Alec! Thank you!" He bounced up and down, hugging me real tight.

"When is this due?"

"I have to turn it in tomorrow."

Really frustrated, I said, "Tomorrow! And you bring it to me at the very last minute?"

"I was tryin' to do it by myself, and I was a little nervous to ask you. I don't wanna fail. So thank you, brother! Really, thank you! It's a persuasive paper. Do you know what that is?"

"Yes," I said. "That's when you must be really convincing in your writing. You have to explain in your own words why you believe something and try to make others believe it. What is the paper about?"

"Why my allowance should be increased. It's a paper to the parents. Tell them why they should give me more money. You can handle that, right?" Antoine didn't even wait for a response. He just left me to get busy.

I stared at the blank piece of paper. Not that I didn't have a ton of ideas to write about, but it just didn't feel right doing Antoine's work.

"What you in there doin'?" Grandma asked, as she stopped at my room door.

Although nothing was on the paper, I covered it up. Right away, I started shaking.

"Boy, now you know you're gonna have to get up real early in the mornin' to pull the wool over my eyes. I been livin' on this here Earth a long time, and I know your brother is tryin' to get you to do his work. I heard y'all talkin' earlier. You told him no. I just was surprised when he made you change and say yes. That's not the Alec I know and helped raise."

At that moment, my body froze. She knew he had asked me to cheat. I was caught.

The only thing I could say was, "I didn't know how to say no, Grandma. Antoine was makin' me feel really bad for him. If he fails, that would be terrible. He made a good point. He doesn't ask me for much. I know it's wrong, but . . . "

Squinting her eyes, she said, "There's no but . . . you know that's wrong."

71

"Are you gonna tell Dad?"

"That's your business, and I'm not even gonna tell you not to do his work. That's your decision too. We all have to learn to make good choices. That's why I'm so glad that you have God in your heart. When you know He's always watchin', you'll do the right thing." She held out her arms to hug me.

"Thanks, Grandma," I said, as I got up and hugged her. Right then, I knew I couldn't continue.

When I walked into Antoine's room, he was playing a video game and smiling like he didn't have a care in the world. He wasn't even trying to do his work. Why should he? He told me to do it.

I simply said, "I'm sorry, but I'm not gonna do your paper."

"You'll be sorry, Alec. Not helpin' me, you really messed up this time."

"My offer still stands if you want me to read somethin' over or help you come up with ideas. But I'm not gonna do your work for you," I told him.

"Get out!" he yelled.

The tears that welled up in his eyes earlier started pouring out. I couldn't help him. Regardless of how he felt, I had to do the right thing.

● ● ●

Valentine's week finally arrived. The fifth grade had been waiting patiently because we had planned a big dance for our fundraiser. The girls came to school wearing their party dresses. And, although the boys said we weren't going to make a big deal out of it, many of us were wearing our good pants and shirts. Some even had on ties. All of us were excited.

"I know we're not gonna be able to hang out with you at the dance," Trey teased. "You're gonna be dancin' with Morgan all afternoon."

Zarick spoke up, "Yeah, whatever Morgan tells him to do, he'll be doin'."

I didn't like that they were teasing me. But I was tough and no girl was going to tell me what to do.

To hush them up quickly, I said, "I'll be workin' at the dance and won't have time to do anything else."

"We'll see," Trey replied, nodding his head.

When Trey went back to his seat, Zarick leaned in and said, "You'd better make time to dance with Morgan, or someone else will."

I knew he was talking about himself because at the beginning of the school year, he tried to get Morgan to like him. Between him and me, she leaned more my way. And, for some reason, I really care a lot for her. However, the whole school didn't need to know it, so I had to be cool.

Later, when we were at the dance I was collecting the money at the door with Coach Braxton. Morgan walked over and greeted me, "Hey, Alec."

"Hey," I said, halfway wanting to speak.

Now I really did want to speak but again there were

people looking at us. I couldn't just act all excited. The kids would tease me forever if the fellas saw me acting too giddy.

She came closer and said, "Can I help you? I'm on the student counsel. I'm allowed to take money."

Being firmer than necessary, I replied, "You're the secretary. You don't have to take notes today."

She looked at me really weird. Coach looked at me like I was crazy too. I wanted to take back those words, but I had already said them.

"Okay. Maybe later we can dance or somethin'."

Instead of giving her an answer, I just started coughing. Morgan walked away.

Coach Braxton said, "Son, she seems like a sweet young lady. Why did you act like you don't want to dance with her? I thought you were smart. What made you pass up a chance to cut a rug with her?"

I squinted. "Cut a rug? I don't know what you mean, sir. The floor is wood."

"That's what folks my age used to say."

When Coach started dancing to the music, the kids looked at him, and everyone started laughing. I didn't know if he was trying to be extra funny or if that's how he really dances. Whichever one, he didn't need to be doing that. But he didn't seem to care.

Once everybody arrived, I didn't have to man my station at the door any longer. To keep from looking like I was hanging out with a girl, I stood against a wall and watched the crowd. Morgan couldn't get upset because it looked like I was making sure everything was all right. It would be sort of like doing safety patrol duty at the dance or something.

Then Trey, Zarick, Billy, and some other guys took up post beside me. We were all standing there with our arms folded. Our heads were tilted and we were eyeing the girls as they danced with each other.

When the next song started to play, Morgan kept waving at me to get my attention. Although I should have waved back because I actually wanted to dance with her, it felt like something had my feet on lock down.

"Lord," I prayed. *"I'm struggling here. I don't want to be called out as a wimp. But I actually like that I like Morgan, even though part of me is against it. I'm all confused. Please make this hurry and be over. I just wanna get through this dance really fast. Can You make time fly right now? Help. Amen."*

Looking around the room for something else to do, there was nothing. I didn't need to man the refreshments because some teachers were handling that. We hired a DJ to play music, and he had the place rocking. There was nothing for me to do.

Dr. Richardson came over to us boys and said, "You all get out there on the floor and dance. If you don't want to dance with the girls then dance with each other."

We looked at her like she had lost it. Then she said, "You know, we can all do the electric slide. I'll tell the DJ to put the music on."

Usually, Dr. Richardson was so professional. To hear her acting all excited was cool. Everything was fine until Morgan walked over to remind me, "So you said maybe later we could hang out. It's later. Are you ready to dance now?"

Morgan's arm was extended toward mine. Although she looked pretty, I didn't want to be embarrassed by all eyes being on us.

Billy, one of the guys next to me, spoke up and said, "I know you're not gonna leave us hangin' and dance with a girl. Ewww!"

"Of course, he is," added Trey. "I already told ya. Anything Morgan says to do, he's gonna do it. Isn't that right, Zarick?"

Zarick said nothing, and that was all he needed to say because the ball was in my court. Basketball is my sport. Right now, this felt like a moment when my team was behind by two points. We could win the game if I make the three-point shot.

As though I was behind the line, I imagined myself tossing the ball up in the air. Then, I said, "Naw, I'm not dancin'." For me, that moment felt like the ball hit the rim and didn't go in.

Morgan looked at me with sadness in her eyes. Then her look turned to anger and her eyes filled up with tears.

"I can't believe you're not gonna dance with me, Alec," she cried. "I know it's probably because you're tryin' to impress these stupid boys."

Before she could get too far away, Zarick ran up to her and said, "I'll dance with you."

Then all the guys around me said the same thing. "You can dance with me! No, you can dance with me! No me. No me!"

They were all hitting me in the head and on the arm. The whole thing made me feel so small. There was no use in going up to Morgan to apologize. Major damage had already been done. She didn't dance with anybody. She didn't even stay at the dance. That's just how bad I had embarrassed her.

I stood there wondering, *Now, what do I do?*

● ● ●

Okay, I couldn't take it any longer. So I just made up my mind to go after Morgan. I couldn't let her think I didn't care. She needed to know that I did, and that I was sorry for acting so dumb. I went out into the hall and saw her coming out of the girls' restroom.

"Hey," I said in a really sweet tone.

Morgan wasn't having it. She snapped her fingers and rolled her neck. I'd never seen her that upset with me.

With her hands on her hips, she said, "Please, don't even *hey* me."

"Morgan, just let me apologize," I said to her, as she walked right by me and headed toward the door.

"My mom is on her way to pick me up. I can't show my face in there anymore when I was embarrassed by someone I thought actually cared."

"We can go back to the dance and you can tell me off in front of everybody. Don't be mad at me. Don't leave the dance."

"Just tell me why, Alec? Can you explain why you did me so wrong? You acted like we're all cool with my grandparents at the play and dinner."

Then she screamed at the top of her lungs. "I don't even wanna talk to you anymore? Just leave me alone!"

"Hey, hey, hey! What is this? What is going on over here?" Dad came out of his office and into the hallway when he heard the loud talking.

Morgan and I just looked at each other. Then, when I looked back at my dad, he was sort of shaking. There were tears in his eyes. I figured it was because he was tired from working too long.

But Dad said, "Alec, we've got to go now, son. I was just going to the cafeteria to get you."

"But I wanna stay and dance with Morgan."

Morgan spoke up, "You had your chance to dance with me and you passed it up." Right then, she made me feel smaller than an ant. "'Bye, Dr. London."

After that, she headed to the front door. I just threw my hands up in the air. This was not good.

"Daaadddd," I groaned, "I was tryin' to work things out with her."

"Work things out? Son, come on. We have to leave."

"But just let me talk to Morgan."

"Son, we must go now!" Dad said more forcefully. Now, it was plain to me that something was seriously wrong. It wasn't just that he was tired.

His cell phone rang as we were walking out of the school. Morgan was waiting by the door, but she turned her back to me and folded her arms. I had messed up pretty good and this wasn't going to be an easy fix.

Just then, Dad got my attention with his conversation over the phone.

"Yeah, honey. I don't know what's going to happen this time. We're headed over there now. Just pray, that's all I can say."

"Dad, what's goin' on?" I asked, immediately after he ended the call. Now, I had to know what was happening.

"Grandma's in the hospital, son," he replied. He unlocked the car door and we both got in.

There were about a million questions to ask, but Dad had other things on his mind. So I decided to keep quiet until we were in a thirty-five-mile zone and he was going sixty. Before I could tell him to slow down, we heard a siren behind us. He hit the steering wheel very hard.

Pulling over to the curb, Dad said loudly, "Oh, no. I don't need this now!"

I just started praying, *Lord, my father's frustrated because something's going on with my grandmother. I don't know, but You do. Please help him to calm down.*

"Open the glove compartment, Alec, and hand me that leather case. It holds my insurance card."

"Why do you need that, Dad? I thought you just needed a license to prove you're able to drive."

"Yes, but you also have to show proof of insurance. If I were to hit somebody, I would need to have a way to take care of the damages. Even though I didn't get into an accident now, it's still a requirement to drive."

I opened the compartment, spotted the case, and handed it to my father. He rolled down his window, and an officer with a not-too-happy look on his face came up to the car.

"Sir, you were driving way over the speed limit. I need to see your license and insurance card. Do you know what the limit is? Did you see the sign posted?" the policeman asked.

"Officer, I'm sure I was going too fast, and I am very sorry."

"It's thirty-five, Dad." I leaned over and whispered.

"My son says it's thirty-five," Dad said, as he handed the officer his identification.

"Yep, your son is right. I have a boy too. We sure need to be a good example and lead them properly."

Humbly, my dad said, "We certainly do, sir. My error."

He looked at my father's information. "Dr. London. Wait, you're the principal at my kid's school."

"I guess that's me, officer. You caught me, and for sure it's my mistake. If you'd be so kind as to write me a ticket, please, I'll be on my way. I am in a hurry. I will slow down, but I'm in a hurry."

"Where are you going so fast?"

"My mother was just rushed to the hospital, sir."

"Oh, I'm sorry to hear that, Dr. London. I'll give you a warning this time, but please slow it down. Do you need a police escort there? Or will you be okay?"

"I'm sure I will, we're not too far away. I'll slow it down, officer. I promise."

"Good, sir, and thank you for everything you've done to turn our school around. My son is really learning a lot. He's just in the fourth grade, but I can see a big difference in the last couple of years since you've been there."

"Well, thank you for that. But I do deserve a ticket."

"Well, today I'm going to bless you instead. Your leadership has surely blessed our family."

"I appreciate that."

"Wow, Dad, that was really nice," I said, as we got back on the road.

I could tell my father was out of it. He was trying to hold back tears and not show me how upset he really was. He was being really strong.

I put my hand on his shoulder and said, "Dad, I love you. I'm your son. I know you love Grandma. It's okay."

"Yeah, it's just hard. I thought she was going to have more time."

As soon as we got to the hospital, Aunt Dot came rushing up to us. Putting her arms around Dad, she said, "The cancer spread. I just don't know. She might not come out of the hospital this time."

My grandmother was in the intensive care unit, and there can only be two visitors at a time. Besides I couldn't go because you have to be at least twelve. On the way to the hospital, Aunt Dot had picked up Antoine. When he came back from seeing Grandma, he rushed over and hugged me.

"What are we gonna do without her, man? How are we gonna make it?" My tough brother actually broke down in my arms.

This was really hard because I didn't want to lose my grandmother either. One Sunday when I went to church with her, Grandma's pastor said that when we die, we go home to be in heaven with the Lord. When I asked her about it, she told me that is good news for believers. That's why we don't have to fear death.

Yes, it was going to be a good thing for my grandmother, but it wasn't going to be a good thing for us. We would all miss her so much. What could I say to my brother who was in my arms, crying his eyes out? He had just seen our grandmother looking so frail. There were no words I could say that would take away his hurt feelings and make him feel better.

Letter to Mom

Dear Mom,

Okay, so being me isn't easy. I probably shouldn't tell you all of this, but since you've gone back to LA, I will. Your other son, Antoine, is tripping. Mom he wanted me to write his paper for him. I was going to do it, but Grandma overheard us talking about it and she made me realize it was the wrong thing to do. So I told Antoine I wouldn't do it, and then he got super mad at me.

He's not the only son of yours who did something wrong. At our Valentine's Day dance, I was mean to Morgan because I didn't want the boys to tease me. I feel bad that I hurt her feelings, but I feel worse that Grandma is back in the hospital. I'm scared we may lose her, Mom.

Pray for me and for Grandma.

Your son,
Nervous Alec

Word Search:

Top Olympic Teams

The ultimate level of track and field is playing for your country in the Olympics and winning a medal. Below are some of the top teams in the world.

```
Y  A  O  V  U  F  B  N  K  G  A  Q
G  N  Q  I  N  Z  Q  V  A  R  C  Q
A  J  A  H  I  X  G  U  D  E  I  D
E  T  I  M  F  P  S  A  N  A  A  U
A  C  U  R  R  T  D  I  A  T  M  M
U  S  A  P  R  E  C  L  L  B  A  M
J  B  R  A  W  A  G  A  N  R  J  O
W  L  L  U  Y  A  M  R  I  I  X  I
C  I  D  N  A  L  N  T  F  T  Y  T
A  C  E  Y  L  N  J  S  E  A  J  Z
V  K  U  Y  E  T  Q  U  L  I  B  L
L  H  I  K  K  L  L  A  P  N  F  Q
```

AUSTRALIA   **FINLAND**   **GERMANY**

GREAT BRITAIN   **JAMAICA**   **KENYA**   **USA**

Real Challenge

5

I was kicking my bed and throwing clothes from my closet onto the floor. It was all because this was too hard to deal with. It had been twenty-four hours since Grandma had gone to the hospital, but it seemed like forever. There was no change in her condition. And the way Dad was moping around, it didn't look like she was going to make it.

"What in the world is all this noise about? What's going on in here?" Mom said, as I heard her jiggling the door knob. When she found out that it was locked, she demanded, "Open up this door this very minute, Alec London!"

I rushed to the door, opened it, and just grabbed her around her waist extra tight. Not knowing she was home, I was completely in shock. It reminded me of when she surprised me and appeared at my karate practice a while ago.

"You're here! You're back! Oh, my goodness. Mom, how did you know I needed you?"

"Alec, honey, your dad told me everything that's going on. I took the first plane home. He's pretty much staying at the hospital, and I know I needed to be here with you boys. When I came in last night, you were sleeping, and I didn't want to disturb you. Now it's six a.m. on Sunday morning, and I really wanted to sleep in. But with all this noise . . . what's going on, son?"

"She's gonna die, Mom. She's gonna go to heaven. I'm not ready for this. It isn't easy. I don't know how to deal with it."

"I'm here, baby. I'm here. Let it out," Mom said, allowing me to just vent.

"Why? Why does it always have to be something going wrong? I like Grandma so much. She got sick last year and pulled through. Why do we have to die anyway? I can't even sleep, Mom. I just thought about myself dying one day and couldn't take it. I can't breathe. If God loves us so much then why does life hurt so bad?"

We sat on the edge of my bed, and she rocked me as I cried. This was hard.

Mom explained, "There're lots of things that the Lord does that we're not going to understand until we're with Him in heaven one day. Honestly, I'm an adult and the mystery of death can sometimes be unsettling when you try to make sense of it all. But the Bible says that God doesn't want us to be afraid of death. Because when we are no longer living in these bodies, then we are in the presence of the Lord. So I rejoice in knowing that someday the Lord

will say to me, "well done, my good and faithful servant."
Then I'll get to see my grandmother and my father again.
And most importantly, I will be with God Almighty."

"So you're not afraid? You're not worried? Are you
ready to die?"

"I want whatever God wants for my life. Am I living
recklessly so I can end my life sooner than He wants? No.
Would I like to be here so I can see my own sons grow up
to be wonderful men who please Him? Of course, I would.
But if I die tomorrow, I'm 100 percent sure that I would be
in heaven because my name is written in the Lamb's Book
of Life."

Mom was making me feel better, especially when she
said, "I have nothing to fear. We just have to live right
while we're here, Alec. I know God's got everything under
control. You have to trust Him and have faith in knowing
that He's capable of healing your grandmother. But if the
end of her life is near, remember it's just the beginning of
her having eternal peace, happiness, and joy with the Lord.
We don't want her to suffer, baby, do we?"

I shook my head no. But honestly, I didn't want to
suffer the pain and agony of missing her terribly either. I
remember when I was in the third grade and we lost a student and his dad in a car accident. He was a boy with special needs and we had just become buddies. In a flash, he
was gone, but I did get through it. At the time, I vowed
never to forget my friend. Now, it's been a couple of years
and I haven't done anything to honor his memory. When

this crisis is over, I'm going to have to change that.

"Mom, you remember my friend Tim?"

"Yes, I do."

"You've got to help me figure out somethin' I can do to keep honoring his memory."

She kissed my forehead and said, "I sure will."

My mom is such an awesome lady. I slid back in my bed and she made sure I was tucked in okay. Somehow I drifted off to sleep with her next to me. I didn't worry because my mother was there. It was like what Mom had just said about trusting that God is with me. I shouldn't fear anything or stress out because I have a heavenly Father whose arms I'm always in.

A little while later, we were awakened by my father. When Mom stepped out of my room to talk to him, I sat up nervously on the edge of my bed, waiting for my parents to tell me something.

Dad came in my room and said, "Good morning, son. Your mom told me that you've really been worried about your grandmother."

"Yeah, Dad, what's goin' on? Is she okay?"

"She's still the same right now, but I need you to toughen up for me. Your mom is here, but I need you to be strong too."

What was I supposed to do? Just act like I didn't care? Act like I had no feelings? Act like this didn't bother me at all? That wasn't how I was feeling inside, and I couldn't act fake about it. This didn't seem like a time to be tough. I didn't want to cry, for sure, but I couldn't help that I was emotional about it. She is my grandmother, and I deeply love her, maybe more than ever before. Wasn't that a good thing? So I just looked away.

As if he could feel my pain, Dad put his hand on my shoulder and said, "All right, son, I understand how you feel. This is all new for me, and I'm worried too, but I can't break down, and I don't want you to either. My mom would want us to be strong. So clean up this room and no more temper tantrums. Okay? Let's keep trusting God."

"Can we pray, Dad?"

"Sure, son. You go ahead."

I started to pray, *"Lord, thank You for my father and for his desire to be strong. Right now, we lift up his mother, my grandmother, who loves You so much. And we just ask that Your will be done and that our desire for You to heal her will happen. But, if not Lord, would You give us what we need to make it through? We love You, and we praise You, in Jesus' name. Amen."*

"Amen, little brother," he teased, as he hugged me briefly and walked out.

I was better because he was right. With God on my side, I could toughen up. I just had to.

● ● ●

"Tyrod, I don't even know why you're in here!" Morgan shouted at the top of her voice. "No one appointed you to this committee."

"Don't be mad at me because I just said y'all ideas are whack," said Tyrod.

"Well, if you don't have anything positive to say . . . " Trey started, before pausing, " . . . you should leave! We're tryin' to plan the end of the year activities, and we can't do that if you're distractin' us."

Tyrod made an ugly face. "Wah wah wah, listen to the little babies."

"You need to leave," Trey called out.

"You can't make me," Tyrod taunted my friends.

This was an after-school meeting gone wrong. I was supposed to be conducting it as the chair. My dad had given me some information on policy and procedures. I was supposed to open the meeting, have an agenda, and make sure that the meeting moved along and stayed on track. Also, I had to make sure all items on the agenda got addressed. If there was something that needed to be voted on, I was to conduct the vote and only cast my vote in the event of a tie. As the chair, my leadership was to remain impartial, and I couldn't take sides.

No one was to speak on the subject more than three times. As I heard my classmates bicker back and forth, I knew that rule was completely broken, but for some reason, I didn't care. I sat there and let them go at it. I mean, we were here to come up with great ideas for our school and our class. If they didn't take that seriously and wanted to argue for no reason at all, then that was on them.

Morgan spoke up and said, "Alec, aren't you gonna do anything about all this? You're the president. And you're just bein' too passive when you should take charge. How did I ever think you were a great person?"

When Morgan stormed off, I just couldn't take it anymore. I got up out of my seat and walked out of the room. I passed by Coach Braxton in the hall and told him I didn't want to lead anymore. When he called out my name a couple times for me to come back, I just kept walking. It didn't matter that I was elected to this position. It didn't matter that my peers thought I could do the job. It didn't even matter that probably if I really tried, I could get things to work out. I kept on walking because I wanted out.

I couldn't go to Dad's office until another twenty minutes passed and the meeting was supposed to be over. Otherwise, it would raise more trouble. If I did that, my dad would ask me way too many questions. Instead, I went back to my classroom, and Dr. Richardson was still there, grading papers.

"Can I just sit in here for a minute?"

"Sure, you may," she corrected me. Dr. Richardson had taught us the grammar lesson on the proper use of *can* and *may*. Use *can* when you're talking about having the ability to do something, and use *may* when you are asking permission to do something. I should have used the word *may*.

"Did your meeting end early?" she asked.

Why did she have to ask me that? I wasn't a liar, so I

couldn't say yes. But I didn't want to talk about it either. I looked away.

Sensing my frustration, my teacher said, "It wasn't a good meeting, huh?"

"No, ma'am."

"I can tell from your distance that you don't want to talk about it. Do you?"

"No, ma'am," I said, hoping she wouldn't press me further.

"Well, I respect that. Since you're in here, though, I'll tell you that I graded your class work from today. You missed most of the math problems. Let me just take a few minutes to go over this material. I know you're having a hard time, but this is important."

So I sat down and she started explaining. "To find the perimeter of a square, you add all four sides."

"I get that, but for some of the problems, only three sides gave a number. On some others, there was only a number on one side. So what do you do?" I asked her, a bit confused.

"Great question. Now I have a question for you. In a square, are all sides equal or are they different?"

I answered, "All sides are equal."

"So if only one side is given, then what are the other sides? The same or different?"

Getting it, I said, "They're the same. Ooh, so if one side is 8 cm, then all sides are 8 cm. And, to find the perimeter, you add $8 + 8 + 8 + 8$."

"Correct, or you can say 4* one side. In this case it's 4*8 = 32."

I went on to do the rest of the problems. Dr. Richardson smiled when she saw me rolling through them. It was easy.

"When you try, Alec London, you're an exceptional student. I know it was because of the difficult time you had last year that you tested out of the gifted program. But I think you need to be back in that class for middle school. However, you can't give half an effort. You have to try all the time, and when you don't understand something, you need to raise your hand."

Although I'd been feeling pretty bad when I first came in, I appreciated her showing me where I messed up. Then she said, "Take the initiative, speak up, and ask questions. Don't just sit back and try to solve problems when you don't know how to do it. It's not like you to miss almost every question. You know that I don't mind going over something again if fundamentally you don't have an understanding."

"Yes, ma'am."

"Think of it this way. If you don't get something, some of the other students probably don't get it either. As I graded the papers, I noticed you weren't alone. I'm glad we went over it now because tomorrow we're going to break up into pairs. I want you to work with some of your class-mates to help them get it."

I huffed.

"Okay, what's wrong with you helping others? You

93

used to do that with no problem."

"I don't know. I'm just tired of everybody putting me up to help folks. Like you said, I missed all the problems myself. I need to be working on me. I don't want to show anybody else the way."

"But, Alec, we went over the problems, and in ten minutes you answered the questions correctly. You've got it now. What's wrong with sharing your knowledge with someone else? It's part of the job of being a leader. That's the Alec London I know."

I didn't respond, but maybe she didn't know me so well. It was a lot of responsibility being a leader, being a smart student, being a chair over a committee, and I just didn't want the responsibility. Was that so bad?

● ● ●

"Mom, do I have to go to track practice? I'm not gonna have that much time with you before you go back to California. I think we should have some mother and son bonding time. Isn't that the stuff you always talk about? Track, I mean it's a waste of my time," I said with a groan. She would have made me happy if we went to get my favorite meal, a burger and fries.

My mother just looked straight ahead and kept driving. She didn't even answer me. When Mom ignored me like that, it meant she had a lot on her mind. She was frustrated and didn't need me to keep bugging her. Eventually, she'd get around to answering my question.

As we pulled into the high school parking lot where we were training, she said, "I'm sorry, son."

"For what, Mom?" I asked, thinking it could be a bunch of things she was talking about.

"Alec, I'm sorry all of this is so hard on you. Over the past week since I've been home, I've seen a dramatic change in you. You're very reserved. You eat and then go to your room. When you come home from school, you stay in your room. You're not riding your bike. You're not hanging out with Morgan. And worst of all, you and Antoine aren't even talking. This isn't what I want for you at all."

I wanted to say, *So if you care about my feelings then why are you making me go to track when I'm telling you it's not something I want to do? Yes, the coach is cool, and he thinks I have a lot of talent. And yes, I met a great high school guy who wants to mentor me. But so what? I want to play football, and I certainly don't want to be on any team with Tyrod. Not an FCA team, not a baseball team, and not a track team.*

But then Mom batted her eyes at me and said, "I really do appreciate you, son. You're handling tough things and pushing through for your father and me. That just means the world to me."

I slowly opened the car door, knowing that I had to be a big boy and just deal with it.

"McDonalds when I pick you up. Okay? Big Mac on me," she promised.

That made me smile just a little, but it wasn't nearly

enough. When I walked onto the track, Tyrod ran back-ward up to me like I was supposed to be impressed that he was coordinated. He wasn't so cool when it came to the books, and I already knew he was athletic. So what?

"I'm surprised you showed up. You left out of the meetin' we elected you to lead the other day. I knew they should've voted me fifth-grade class president. I don't crack under pressure. Now, look at you—you're no leader. Looks like I might get the job anyway," Tyrod taunted me.

Before I could respond, he jogged away. After Coach made us warm up by jogging around the field, doing calis-thenics, and stretching, he called us all over to the bleach-ers. Then he introduced Mr. Derrick Moore again.

"Well, hello again," Mr. Moore said to the group. "I'm super excited to have an opportunity to talk to you guys about the next component of the C.L.I.M.B. principle. Today, we are going to focus on the word *care*."

I didn't want to be rude and roll my eyes in front of the man. He was a big dude who wasn't boring by any means. It was just that the word had nothing to do with how I was feeling on the inside. My thought was, since so much was going wrong, what difference did it make to be concerned about it? But there was no way I could go anywhere. I had to listen, so I tuned in.

Mr. Moore said, "Coach tells me you all aren't giving 100 percent for him. He's trying to help you win the district meet so that you can qualify for state and possibly go on to the junior Olympics. I believe you can do it, but deep inside you've got to check yourself. If you embrace these four principles, you'll find something that kicks in to change you for the better."

Tyrod interrupted. "I don't know about these guys, Mr. Moore, but I'm ready."

The upperclassmen looked back at Tyrod and started laughing.

Mr. Moore said, "For a little guy, you've got spunk. I'll give you that. Even though you think you're ready, partner, check out these nuggets. They can help you stay dynamite, okay?"

"Yes, sir," Tyrod said proudly.

Mr. Moore began, "In order for you to be a leader, you first must be *capable*. Not everyone has the ability to lead, but you're on this elite track team because you have the skills. If you're all leaders, it means you're all going to give 100 percent. Not only are you capable, but when you tap into the gear that shows you're something special, then watch out."

I had to think about what he was saying. I was capable of a lot of things. Capable of being elected class president, capable of having great grades, capable of being on this elite track team. Now that I know I've got the talent, I have to tap into the knowledge. As Mr. Moore said, it's time to operate in it. *Wow,* I thought, *that's real interesting.*

He challenged my thoughts again when he continued and said, "Next, you also need to be *accountable*. It's great to have the skills, but can the coach and your teammates depend on you? If you sign up for anything in life, are you going to follow through with what you said? You're not just going to quit when things get tough. No, that's not being a person of high moral character. Listen, I know, because I'm older than you guys, that life isn't going to be easy. But that's okay. When you stick to what you said you're going to do, you can make it better."

Tyrod looked over at me and started coughing. He knew I had just walked out on the fifth-grade planning meeting. Mr. Moore was on my street. He wasn't worlds away; he was right in my neck of the woods. It was time for me to decide what I was going to do about it.

Mr. Moore continued and said, "Now, you also need to be *reliable*. You have the skills, and you are showing up. But when people rely on you, they expect you not to just be there in body. You also have to be there in soul, heart, passion, and drive. If your teammate is down, can he rely on you to help pick him up? Remember, your team is only as good as your weakest link. That means when a teammate is going through a difficult time, you need to give him encouraging words to help him get better. That way, you all can go on and win."

I looked over at Tyrod, and he was looking down at the floor. Was this talk getting to him too? Maybe he was thinking about it. Instead of bashing me, he could be helping me. But he wasn't doing that. Maybe he knew that was wrong. How interesting.

"And the last thing you need is to *engage*. The same

way that you guys are locked in on me right now," Coach Moore said, "you need to be focused, ready, and excited. Because, if you don't believe you can, you won't. Think about what I'm saying, young people. Be capable, be accountable, be reliable, and be engaged. Care about this track team, and care about all you're doing in life. Care about yourselves."

Everything that he was saying sounded really good. He actually motivated me. I didn't even want to come to practice, but I really needed this talk. It turned on a light in me that was somehow turned off. I needed to care, and now that I wanted to, I took a deep breath. Figuring out how to put it into practice was going to be the real challenge.

Letter to Mom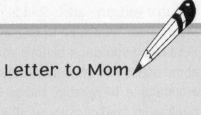

Dear Mom,

You are back. I'm so happy, but it's sad that you're here because of everything going on with Grandma. Really, I am upset that something awful keeps happening in my life. I pray, and things still go wrong.

I don't care about anything. Why should I? It won't matter. I haven't been willing to help anybody. I haven't been motivated to be the fifth-grade class president.

Most of all, I don't want to do track. But I was glad that I went today because a man named Mr. Moore came and said some things I'll think about.

Your son,
Struggling Alec

Word Search:

Division 1 Teams

In the world of college athletics, track and field is a very important sport. Listed below are some of the colleges and universities that usually lead the way in this sport.

```
Y   V   W   O   S   E   I   M   P   U   D   V
S   I   Q   X   Z   T   F   O   B   S   X   P
H   R   M   A   S   A   X   E   T   L   K   S
M   G   B   D   Q   T   B   D   E   V   T   M
W   I   H   F   P   S   Z   V   A   A   A   Q
G   N   R   R   F   A   I   J   N   I   I   A
Q   I   Q   C   O   D   N   F   K   F   Z   R
F   A   W   H   A   I   O   O   K   N   N   B
I   T   W   N   B   R   S   S   Z   U   C   H
J   E   D   Y   D   O   O   H   Y   I   I   Q
T   C   P   K   W   L   G   B   H   M   R   H
I   H   Q   F   A   F   L   M   I   Z   T   A
```

	ARIZONA	BYU	FLORIDA STATE
LSU	STANFORD	TEXAS AM	VIRGINIA TECH

Strong
Willpower

6

"Andre, I told you I'm not going to talk about this anymore. Please, drop it already," Mom said, as she slammed the bedroom door and stormed down the hallway.

My parents had been arguing so loud that Antoine and I were standing by our doorways listening. My brother still wasn't speaking to me. However, I was starting to take in the lessons that we're learning from the C.L.I.M.B Program. Because I truly care for Antoine, I don't want to be his crutch. He just had to deal with being upset. His issue wasn't my fault, and I wasn't going to let him make me feel bad about it.

However, knowing Mom is so upset right now, I do wish I could at least talk to Antoine. I'd like to get my brother's take on all of this. When he saw me looking his way, he rolled his eyes, went right back into his room, and slammed the door.

When Dad heard the noise, he stepped into the hallway

and yelled out, "Who keeps slamming doors around here?"

Instead of pointing to my brother's room, I shrugged my shoulders and went back to my room. Closing the door gently, I sat on my bed and stared at the Bible on my dresser. As I walked over to pick it up, silently I prayed, *"Lord, let me find something that is easy for me to understand. I need a word from You. I have a desire to know You more, trust You more, and just be better. So much around me is crazy. I need Your help."*

I opened my Bible to chapter 4 of the book called Philippians, and verse 13 was at the top of the page. It said that I can do all things through Christ who gives me strength. After reading that verse, a calm feeling came over me. It reminded me of the times when I saw Grandma sitting with a Bible in her hand, smiling from ear to ear. She looked like she had just eaten the best meal ever. Grandma would tell me that she was full and satisfied from God's Word. Now I understood what she was talking about.

God was giving me hope that things were going to be better. And His Word just told me that He would give me the strength to endure whatever comes along. I believe God made me a leader, a helper, a giver, and I have to start acting like that's who I am.

Feeling stronger already, I got up and went to look for my mom. She was in the living room. "Mom, can I talk to you for a sec?" I asked.

Shaking her head, she replied, "Oooh, not right now, honey. I'm getting ready to—"

Cutting her off, I said, "Please, Mom, please."

I went over and hugged her. She looked down at me, and we sat on the couch. When she smiled at me, I knew she was ready to listen. Earlier, I overhead her and Dad say something that I couldn't wait to talk to Mom about. It sounded too good to be true, and I needed to be sure.

"Is it true? Are you back for good? Like, you're not going back to California ever?

She nodded slowly.

"Did the show get cancelled? Did you finish taping? Did you all do a series finale? I don't understand."

She looked away. When she looked back at me, her eyes had little puddles in them. Then, just like water dripping slowly from a faucet, she couldn't hold back her tears.

"Mom, what's wrong?"

"The show is still going, son. I left on my own. I decided after much prayer that this is where I need to be. The Atlanta area is growing when it comes to television entertainment. If it's God's will, I'll find something here. My days of living in California are over."

"But what about your mom?"

"She's thrilled to be connected with my family. She'll be coming out here to visit from time to time. Don't worry."

"So if it's all good, why are you and Dad mad? What's wrong, Mom? Talk to me. Please, you said I'm older, and I'm makin' you proud. Talk to me. Do you resent us because you had to make such a tough choice? If that's the case, Mom, you've gotta go back out there. I don't want you to be mad at us because of this."

She took both of her hands, cupped my face, and said, "You are my priority. My family is my priority. It's natural that this is a difficult decision, but I'll get used to it. Being here is worth it. I'm happy with my choice."

● ● ●

"So when I fail the seventh grade, you know it'll be your fault, little brother," Antoine said to me nastily.

He hadn't talked to me in a couple of weeks. And if he was going to be all yucky about it, I'd actually prefer for him to keep his distance. I gritted my teeth, shifted my eyes, and walked away. My parents were gone to the hospital. I knew Antoine felt that because we were alone, he could just cut up and go off on me. News flash! I wasn't going to stand there and let him talk to me any old kind of way.

Then, as soon as I turned my back, he grabbed my arm and jerked it really hard. "Did you hear what I said? It's your fault that I'm gonna be repeatin' the seventh grade!"

The next thing I knew, he put his fist under my chin and pinned me up against the wall. Honestly, he must have forgotten that I'd been taking karate because my instincts kicked in. With my left hand, I gave him an uppercut. When Antoine reacted, I twisted around and before he knew it, he was pinned up against the wall. The look of shock on his face said, "Man, my little brother's got skills!"

"You need to watch who you're messin' with, Antoine.

I'm not botherin' you, and you can't blame me for your situation. Let's call a spade a spade, I'm not the one in your class every day, half listenin', tryin' to be a class clown, not doin' my homework, not askin' questions to get help, and failin' tests. Bottom line, I'm not the one responsible for you failin' the seventh grade."

I pulled him away from the wall and pushed him into the bathroom. Not even knowing I was that strong, I guess I was so fed up that my strength kicked in.

Pointing his face at the mirror, I told him, "Blame you!" Then I took my hands off of him, fixed my clothes, and walked to my room.

Antoine followed, "Oh, so you think you can just say whatever you wanna say to me, handle me any kind of way, and get all up in my grill? You mean, we're not gonna talk about this thing?"

"Oh, now you wanna talk. After you put your hands all over me, now you wanna talk? Really, Antoine, seriously?" I asked him.

Shock came over me when Antoine just slid down the wall and put his head in his lap. With one elbow, he kept hitting the wall over and over again. He did it so many times until finally, I just held his arm.

"Stop doin' that," I told him.

Jerking away, he said, "Doesn't matter. I'm no good anyway. I'm worthless. I'm not smart like you. Because of my grades, I couldn't play any sports this year. Seventh grade is when you get to play on the school team, and I couldn't even play. You're right, I can't blame you, but it's not like I didn't try. You think all I do in class is cut up and try to be bad? Well, I listened. I just couldn't get it. Okay? Why wouldn't you just help me, Alec? Nobody would've ever known."

I didn't want to tell him that Grandma heard us talking about it. Antoine loves her too, and he'd probably feel really awful if he knew she thought he was trying to cheat. After she made me make my own decision, I told Antoine what I felt inside me. It was the right thing to do.

Maybe this was my chance to share my feelings with him. What could I lose? He'd already been mad at me for a long time. At least, we're talking. It's time to be real.

"I'm a believer. I love the Lord and really wanna please Him. I'm not perfect, so don't look up at me like that. But I do know right from wrong. It would've been wrong for me to write your paper for you. Still, that didn't mean I didn't wanna help. Remember last year when I helped you study? It worked then, didn't it, Antoine? We studied math together, and you got an A on the test. Right?"

"Yeah, so I got math down. It's English that's gettin' me now."

"So you gotta be a well-rounded student."

"What does that mean?"

"It means you have to try hard and be good in all your subjects. That's what Dad keeps tellin' me. I've been struggling, and I have to work extra hard at doing my best too."

"I don't read that well. When I see the letters, sometimes an H looks like a B, and an O looks like an E. I get all confused," Antoine confessed.

That reminded me of a learning disorder I heard about on TV. It's called dyslexia, where people get numbers, letters, and things backward. A lot of kids don't want anyone to know that they have a problem. But if my brother knows that things are blurry and he mixes up things, he should tell our parents so they could look into it. When I reluctantly shared my thoughts about it with Antoine, he didn't shout at me or tell me I was crazy. He smiled.

Shocked, I said, "You'd be okay with askin' Dad to see if somethin's really wrong?"

"Yeah, because I'm really tryin'. Maybe that's what I have, I don't know. The fact that you're willin' to help me figure it out, I guess it means that you really do care. Huh?"

"Of course, I care. You've been the one walkin' around here, not talkin' to me. But I've been prayin' for you."

"I wanna know God like you do, Alec. I don't wanna be so angry all the time. When Grandma goes to heaven, I need to know that I'll see her again."

"All you have to do is open your mouth and tell Jesus that you are sorry for the bad things you've done and ask Him to come into your heart. That's what they told me to do. And ever since then, I've felt like I need to honor Him, obey Him, and do good things for Him."

"Will you help me?"

Okay, so talking to Antoine about his schoolwork was important, but praying with him would change his life. So we held hands, and we talked to God. He wanted to, and I know God heard us.

● ● ●

"Thank you, Alec, for talking to your Mom and me about Antoine. Your brother's been having trouble with studying because he's really struggling with comprehension in school. We got him tested and he does have a slight case of dyslexia, which is probably why we hadn't caught it before now. You helped him, and it shows how much you care. That's amazing," Dad said to me, as we drove to the track a few days later.

"You're welcome, Dad. Can you tell me what I'm volunteering for again?"

"Coach Braxton has some kids with special needs coming today. Your mom told me you've been thinking about your friend Tim. So when Coach asked me if you could come and help out a couple of hours, I said sure. Besides that, I heard you guys have some issues with the fifth-grade planning committee. Maybe you need to get your mind away from all that and focus on helping those who are less fortunate. It might put a lot of things in perspective for you. You okay with that?" Dad explained.

Without even thinking this was forced on me and I couldn't say no, I had no problem with it. I was actually glad to do it because he was right. Being around special needs kids would make me think about Tim's short life and how he always gave everything he had. Tim never stopped trying because he had a disability. He had passion and a purpose, and I needed to be encouraged by his life.

When we got to the field, I was surprised when my dad got out of the car.

"You're not goin' to the hospital, or back home, or somewhere else?"

"No, I'm here to see my old high school teammate, Derrick Moore."

"You know the man who's been givin' us the encouraging talks?"

"Yeah, we went to school together down in Albany, Georgia. That's my boy. Here he is right now," Dad said, as Mr. Moore walked over to us.

"Doctor London! What's up, man?" Mr. Moore said, super excited to see my dad.

"Hey, Derrick," Dad said, as they slapped hands. "You've met my son Alec."

"Yeah, but I didn't know that he was your son. He's always so attentive," Mr. Moore said, as he looked at me and winked.

That was a little embarrassing. Even though I've been getting a lot from Mr. Moore's talks, sometimes I didn't want to hear them. I was glad he couldn't tell though. It was cool that my Dad knows a former NFL player. As the two of them were catching up, out of the corner of my eye, I saw a person in a wheelchair who was stuck in a pothole.

I jogged over to her and said, "Hey, my name is Alec. Can I push?"

"Su . . . sure, Alec. I'm Liberty. I . . . I'm in the race today. Ple . . . please push me to the starting line."

As I pushed the girl who was excited about giving her all to race, I looked over and saw two people headed our way. Then they smiled and turned back. I think it must have been her parents because they were waving and saying thanks to me.

Not really thinking I'd done anything big, but just being with Liberty fired her up even more. She kept talking about the race and how she'd been looking forward to it and training really hard. Liberty said it didn't matter if she won or lost. She was just happy to get a chance to participate.

When I got her to the line, I met her competition. They didn't greet each other with fierce intention. And because their hands were slightly deformed, they couldn't give a fist bump the way that I'm familiar with it. They did it their own way, by letting their wrists lightly tap each other.

Liberty said, "You gonna win, James."

James smiled and replied, "No, you gonna win, Liberty."

"No, you gonna win," she said again.

James responded, "No, you gonna win."

Finally, they busted out laughing. Another person going up against them rolled up. He introduced himself to me as Craig.

Craig looked at them and said, "No, I'm gonna beat you both."

The three of them laughed as if they've known each other for years. I was smiling and watching them. For a moment, I'd forgotten they had special needs. It was extraordinary to see how much they cared for each other.

Then, at the same time, as if they'd done this before, the three of them said, "We tie!"

I'm a tough boy, but honestly, it got a little emotional for me to watch them. At first, I wished they had legs like mine, so they could get up out of those wheelchairs and run. However, as I listened to the three of them talking, I realized that they had something way more important. They had heart. I definitely understand now why it's called Special Olympics. They were an awesome group.

It was time for the competitors to get ready for the race. Coach Braxton asked me to step back, but for some reason it was hard to leave them. I was glad to be a part of their moment.

Mr. Moore was standing behind me. He surprised me when he said, "They're amazing to watch, aren't they?"

I looked back and replied, "Yes, sir."

Just then, the whistle blew and off they went.

Everyone cheered as we watched the race. Then Mr. Moore said, "Alec, I've noticed a couple of times when I've been with the group that you looked a little distracted."

He caught me off guard because he had told my dad that I was always paying attention. Seeing the surprised look on my face, he explained, "I didn't want your old man to trip, so I had your back. I know your dad. You come from good stock. From what Coach says about you, you've got awesome potential. I know it might seem like people are on you really hard, but embrace that. The fastest time always comes from the strongest person. When I was coming up, I wasn't the fastest, the most talented, or the strongest one. However, I always worked the hardest."

Mr. Moore's words were so encouraging to me. He finished by telling me, "If you add your talent to your hard work ethic, you'll go far in this life. You could choose the field of athletics or the field of academics. The sky's the limit for you. Just look at those kids out there giving 100 percent. And remember this, you have no physical limitations. You're blessed beyond measure. Now go on and soar. Take the lead, do your best, and tap into your strong willpower."

Letter to Mom

Dear Mom,

Wow! You're staying home for good! Mom, thank you! I know it was a hard decision, but I'm glad you said it's the decision you wanted to make.

Antoine and I talked, and now he understands the decision I made not to cheat for him. I'm happy he got checked for dyslexia too. He wants to do well in school, and I'm glad he's getting the help he needs. Hopefully, it will make a big difference.

Also, today was an eye opener for me as I watched kids with special needs give their all. It taught me that I have to press on too. God is good, and He has given me some great gifts I must use.

Your son,
Thankful Alec

Word Search:

HBCU Teams

(Historically Black Colleges and Universities Teams)

There are four major HBCU athletic conferences. They are the following: Southern Intercollegiate Athletic Conference (SIAC), Mid-Eastern Athletic Conference (MEAC), Southwestern Athletic Conference (SWAC), and the Central Intercollegiate Athletic Association (CIAA). Below are some of the top schools that are great in the sport of track and field.

```
Y  U  E  W  R  F  C  U  T  Q  X  M
F  F  T  K  P  N  I  I  L  M  O  Y
M  A  A  D  I  R  O  L  F  R  Z  V
C  W  T  D  I  U  G  W  E  X  I  I
W  J  S  O  R  D  H  H  X  Y  K  R
T  F  Y  B  A  A  O  G  A  G  B  G
L  T  N  I  F  U  W  A  A  W  T  I
E  T  A  T  S  K  L  O  F  R  O  N
C  W  B  E  A  L  E  Q  H  D  Z  I
X  T  L  H  O  N  Z  G  R  J  B  A
L  F  A  P  C  R  V  C  S  I  J  S
J  O  H  N  S  O  N  C  S  M  B  T
```

ALBANY STATE   FLORIDA AM   HOWARD

JOHNSON CSM   MOREHOUSE   NORFOLK STATE   VIRGINIA ST

Great
Day

7

"**Alec, I'm so** proud of you," Dr. Richardson said when she came to my desk. "Look at your grade!"

I flipped over my paper and saw in big numbers: 100! Also written across the top was an A+. I was fired up. I had studied, and it paid off.

The school day was over, and I was getting ready to go to the planning meeting. Ever since I walked out of an earlier meeting, it had been hard to go to them. Although I'd been attending the meetings the last couple of weeks, I still wasn't taking charge, I was just sort of there. Basically, my dad wouldn't let me quit, and now I wanted things to be better. Truly, I was a little sad about it all.

Dr. Richardson picked up on that when she said, "Okay, you have an A+ and there's a frown on your face. What is wrong, young man? You've got so much going for you. You were elected class president. After you and Zarick became friends, his grades started improving. Before he left, he told me that it was because you encouraged him.

Now, you're pulling A + s. I'm so proud of you."

Feeling undeserving, I said, "Maybe I'm just not cut out to lead. I don't want to go to this meeting."

"You have about ten minutes until it starts. Sit down. Let me tell you a quick story. Your dad once told me that anytime I needed to drop a good word on you, I should do it. Have you ever heard the story of Moses?"

"No, ma'am," I said. "I think he did something great with the sea, but I don't know the story."

Dr. Richardson began, "Moses was one of God's people. They were called the children of Israel. Moses was a good man with a big heart. The Pharaoh, he was like the king of Egypt, wanted to hurt God's children. So the Lord called Moses to lead His people out of Egypt. It wasn't a couple of people, not twenty people, but thousands of people. And they didn't have a lot of time to get out. So the children of Israel followed Moses."

I wanted to understand more about God's Word. Every time I've heard a Bible story, it has helped me. I hoped the story of Moses would do the same. So Dr. Richardson told me where to find it in the Bible.

"The story of Moses is in the book of Exodus, but the part where Moses leads the people out of Egypt is in chapters twelve through fifteen."

I wrote that in my notebook.

Dr. Richardson continued, "See, Alec, the Pharaoh didn't believe in God Almighty, and Moses knew Pharaoh wanted to do the wrong thing. So Moses told God if He wanted him to lead, God had to show him how and give him what he needed. God assured Moses that He would be with him. Then Moses stepped out on faith, and the people followed. Along their journey, it got rough but Moses kept on believing God was with them. Just like in your life, Alec, sometimes when it gets hard, you still hold on to your faith. Right? Then, when Moses and the people reached the Red Sea, they couldn't go any farther."

That made sense to me. The water was blocking them from passing. I wondered where Moses and the people could go with the sea in their way."

My teacher knew the answer. "They couldn't cross over the water so they chilled out, and Moses waited on God to show them the way."

It was a really interesting story. "What happened next?" I asked.

"Alec, I'm telling you, it's awesome. Moses kept his trust in God, and he didn't give up. He knew God would do something big to help him. That's called standing on faith. So Moses got the word that Pharaoh was coming with his army to capture the children of Israel. The people were upset with him and asked him if he'd brought them out there to be killed by Pharaoh. But Moses told them, 'Don't be afraid, stand firm. Watch, and let's see what the Lord is going to do.'"

I was sitting on the edge of my seat, waiting to hear what happened next. "Then," Dr. Richardson continued, "here's the amazing part. God told Moses to hold out his big stick, called a staff, over the water, and the Red Sea opened up. God's great power made the waters divide in half! All of His people were able to walk through the path between the water. Then, just before Pharaoh's army could follow them, the water caved in and the army drowned in the sea. They didn't make it across, but Moses and the people were already on the other side. You see, they trusted God, and God showed up. I'm telling you, Alec, trust Him, and He's going to help you too."

I stood up. I was fired up and ready to be a leader. I went into that meeting and took charge.

● ● ●

It was the day of our first track meet and I was stretching and warming up. When I had to participate in baseball, I didn't like it. But I really do like track after all. Running the 100-yard dash and sprinting as fast as I could was a good feeling. It felt awesome.

Unlike football, where the players have to depend on their teammates to block for them, or for someone to catch the ball, track was different. Yeah, in the case of relay races, track is a team sport, and all of the individual scores contribute to a win. Other than that, most races are won by one person. So if I used my ability to do the best I could, gave my all, and pushed myself, then I'd have a chance to win.

"Can I stretch with you?" a familiar voice said that truly surprised me.

I didn't need to look up. I knew it was Tyrod, but I had

to look up to make sure I wasn't imagining things. Why would he want to stretch with me? It just was crazy.

"What's the catch?" I said, being honest.

"I don't know. A lot of the talks Mr. Moore's been givin' us got to me. He actually pulled me off to the side last week, and we had a real man-to-man. He wants to be my mentor, and I know I've gotta change."

Deep inside I was thinking, *Yeah, you definitely need to change.* But I was really surprised that he was talking about changing.

"If you're serious, Tyrod, and not tryin' to pull my leg, then come on."

As soon as he bent down and began to stretch, he started talking. "You know, we've gotta give it our all today, right? I hear these guys are really good, and we wanna get out the gate strong. We need to win the first meet. I don't know if they really are as good as people say, but when we're runnin' the forty-yard dash, I'm gonna try and beat you. Then you try and beat me too, and we'll definitely beat them. We can do this. Just don't let up like you have been."

Frowning, I said, "What do you mean? I don't let up."

"Yeah right, a couple of times you haven't been givin' your all in practice. You've been lettin' me win."

"No, you've really stepped up your game. You're very good at this. Maybe it was a fluke when we were runnin' at school that day and I won."

"Some of the older guys showed me some techniques.

Coach Braxton did too, so I'm really tryin' to get every edge I can," said Tyrod.

He was taking me by surprise. It was just the fact that he was talking to me in a serious way.

Then Tyrod said, "I can teach you what they taught me. You probably don't wanna learn it today. It might confuse you, but they changed my runnin' stance and everything."

I wasn't expecting a guy who's always acted like we could never be friends to all of a sudden want me to do better. Standing up and folding my arms, I looked straight at him.

"What?" he said. "It's weird, huh, me talkin' to you like this?"

"Yeah, it's like you're supposed to be mean," I said to him.

"But being mean isn't really who I wanna be. I've always wanted to be your buddy, just didn't know how. You didn't wanna connect with me, so I just started acting up, acting out, acting bad, and acting crazy. When Zarick was in our class, it was a new year. I finally thought I could have a best buddy, but he thought you were really cool. Then I started makin' stuff up so he wouldn't like you. I know I was wrong now, so I guess it's been good for me to be alone. That's when I figured out I'm my biggest problem. Talkin' to Mr. Moore has really helped me. I was able to share with him that deep down, more than anything, I want what you've got."

"I have friends because I care about them, not because I try to control them."

"I understand that now. But I also got on you and teased you about being a daddy's boy. Honestly, man, if my dad was just here for me, I would wanna be his boy too."

That's when it finally hit me. I remembered seeing Tyrod's mom once, but I never knew that his dad wasn't in his life at all. Of course, we never talked about stuff like that. But I know how hard it was for me not having my mom around so much of the time. I could only imagine how tough it would be not to have my dad in my life every day.

Then I remembered my cousin, Lil' Pete, and how jealous he was of my brother and me because Dad is in our lives. So much of the question about why Tyrod acted so badly was finally answered. It wasn't an excuse for him to keep being bad, but it certainly was understandable. He was hurt by a person who was supposed to love him the most.

Seeing him sad, I put my hand on his shoulder and said, "It's your dad's loss."

Tyrod looked away, showing the first real sign of emotion that I had ever seen in this guy. His eyes watered up. There was no mistake, he was really down.

To encourage him, I said, "Mr. Moore told me somethin' too. He said you've gotta believe and know you're gonna be awesome. Tyrod, you're gonna live your life in such a way that your dad is gonna wish that he would've been a part of it. Besides, trust me, my dad would be glad to help out. Anytime you wanna hang out and have him take you somewhere, he would love it. He's the principal of our school, and he really cares."

We both noticed the other team members were starting to arrive. They were jogging real fast, and they weren't too small either. Nope, they looked ripped and ready.

I looked over at Tyrod and saw he hadn't pulled himself together yet. I gave him his words back and told him, "Remember, you're gonna try and beat me, and I'm gonna try and beat you. And together, we're gonna beat them, partner."

Tyrod smiled. We shook hands. I couldn't believe we had actually connected.

"I don't even know how to say I'm sorry," he said to me.

"You don't have to," I said back to him, understanding what it was like to do people wrong.

I knew how it felt to take things out on people when you were going through something yourself. Tyrod deserved grace. In fact, it reminded me that I owed Morgan an apology.

"You think we could be friends?" he asked me.

I smiled and said, "Sure."

"Well, come on, let's go win the meet!"

We started running and then he stopped and said, "I'm sorry, Alec."

"I already told you. You didn't have to—"

"Yeah, but just the fact that you're acceptin' me has really made my day."

GREAT DAY

My day was made when we won our first meet. Coach Braxton was super happy. Dad was proud. When he gave Tyrod a fist bump and a hug, I could see in my classmate's eyes that he really needed male mentors to care. In my dad and Mr. Moore, he had them. Maybe now my father could ease up off of me. Then again, knowing how much Dad cares about me, that wasn't going to happen.

● ● ●

"Hey, Alec, good mornin'!" Zarick said, as he stood at my door.

"Hey! What are you doin' here?"

"My mom talked to your parents and they're lettin' me come to your graduation today."

"But aren't you gonna miss school?"

"There's a teacher work day today and we've got a couple of days until we graduate. I'm just excited to be here with you guys," Zarick explained.

I was still stunned.

"What, you're not happy to see me?" he asked. "I wanna hear the speech you're gonna give today."

"Zarick, why don't you come on in and eat some breakfast? Alec, hurry up so you won't be late," Mom called to us.

My friend came in and went straight to the kitchen table where she was already preparing him a breakfast plate. I headed to my room to finish getting ready. When Dad was coming down the hall, he gave me a high five like it was going to be a great day. I just smiled at him.

A little while later when I came into the kitchen, I smiled even wider when I saw him kiss Mom and say, "I'll meet you guys at the school."

"That's great, honey. It'll be so exciting," she said to him.

"What's gonna be exciting, Mom?" I asked, trying to figure out what she was talking about.

She patted my head. "Later, babe, now hurry up and eat your breakfast."

Zarick and Antoine were already eating and laughing a lot. As usual, Mom made a great breakfast, but I felt a little queasy in my stomach. I didn't know if I was worried about all our plans coming together, or if it was my speech that was making me so nervous. Whatever the reason, I wasn't feeling calm at all.

Antoine stopped joking for a minute and said to me, "You know, um, we're proud of you. Right?"

"No."

He turned over a sheet of paper that was lying next to him on the table. On top of it was a grade of B –. I was so thrilled for him that my uneasy feeling went away for a second.

"Because you told me I could do it, I tried, and it worked. I'm proud of you because you helped me know that I had it in me. And I'm proud of you because today you're givin' a speech to your class. I wish that would've been me a long time ago, but I'm gonna try for eighth-grade president next year. You are encouraging to me, little brother," Antoine said, as he tried to pat my head.

● ● ●

A couple of hours later, I was sitting in my chair, waiting to go up on the stage. The room was packed, and my hands were sweaty. When Dr. Richardson stood up to give the opening remarks, Morgan looked at me and saw that I was shaking.

She leaned over and said, "You can do this."

"I'm so sorry I acted so mean to you."

"I'm not mad. I talked with my granddad, and he explained sometimes boys do dumb things. You're still one of my best buddies, Alec. That's not gonna change," she said, as we both smiled at each other.

Dr. Richardson called Morgan up next to give the welcome. I looked around the room and was surprised when I didn't see my father anywhere. Since he's the principal of the school, he really shouldn't be late. I saw Mom waving at me from the audience, and Antoine was sitting next to her making faces. He was a middle school student sitting in the elementary school graduation. I guess he thought that was funny. Zarick was sitting next to them, giving me a thumbs-up.

Just when I was about to get up to go on stage, I turned around again and saw my father near the doorway. He was coming through the crowd, pushing a lady to the front row. I did a double take and saw the person in the wheelchair was my grandmother. She was sitting a little slumped over, but she was there! I walked up to the podium, standing straight and tall.

With confidence that I had something important to say and faith that God would help me get through my nerves, I said, "Today is a wonderful day because there are one hundred and two fifth graders who reached a milestone in their lives. As president of the fifth-grade class, I want to thank our parents for always being there, pushing us to do better, teaching us how to be good team players, and helping us to understand that we can win any battle in life. I also want to thank all of the teachers and administrators here at this great school for letting us know we could go the distance. They believed in us and helped us to achieve greatness."

Nearing the end of my speech, I was feeling strong and confident in what I had to say next, so I continued. "And lastly, to all my fellow classmates . . . our school set the bar high for us, and we've reached excellence. We're graduating from the fifth grade, and now it's time to raise the bar up another level as we move on. I learned some things myself, and if I can pass them on to you, I hope they'll help you too. Remember to always do what's right, be the bigger person, help others, try hard in your studies, and take the lead in your life. Congratulations!"

Everyone stood to their feet and started clapping. It was amazing. I took my seat.

Looking out across the auditorium, there was an air of anticipation. Now we were ready for the big moment when our names would be called. One by one, we came across the stage and Dr. London, my dad, presented us with a rolled up certificate with our names on it. When he handed me my diploma, I was beaming with pride.

After the ceremony was over, my parents told me that they were so proud of the way I gave my speech. Grandma simply cried and kept wiping her tears with a handkerchief. Seeing her there really melted my heart. Antoine patted me on my back extra hard, but when he smiled, I knew it was his way of being in my corner.

After all the family warmth and congratulations, Trey and Morgan stood near me. It was time to start the carnival fun. So I made the announcement that our class was waiting to hear.

Based on the fifth-grade planning committee's request, the school hired a company to bring carnival rides, snow-cone machines, popcorn, hotdogs, and game boards. Everyone was ready to celebrate.

Later on the playground, there was so much excitement. While all the kids were having a great time, Tyrod was sitting alone off to the side. Zarick didn't go to our school anymore and people were glad to see him, but no one was paying Tyrod any attention. I'd be the first one to admit that he deserved it, but this was a new day.

"Didn't you guys hear my speech?" I said to my friends. "Don't you know we're supposed to lend a helpin' hand? Would you want to be sittin' alone right now? Let's all be leaders and include everybody."

Trey called for Tyrod to join us. I could tell from the look on Tyrod's face that he was so excited for the invitation to join in the fun. The boy who had given me trouble for far too long told me thanks. Seeing how much he appreciated being accepted, made me realize mean Tyrod was gone for good.

When my parents motioned for me to come to them, I gladly jogged over. Mom hugged me real tight, and Dad said, "You're learning how to take the lead, son. I'm super proud. Now your Mom's got some good news for you."

"Mom, what is it? You're goin' back to the show?"

"It's good news, son. I just got hired on a show here."

"No way, Mom!" I said, hugging her tighter than a shoe fitting two sizes too small.

She kissed my forehead and said, "I'll have some crazy working hours, but I'll have a lot of free time too."

I hugged both of my parents, and my brother gave me five. Morgan looked over and smiled just to see me happy. Quietly, I told the Lord, *"Thanks."*

This was a terrific day, and I was a young man who'd learned a lot. Life isn't always going to bring great times, but as long as you have faith in God and are good at heart—things will work out.

As I looked at Tyrod, Zarick, Morgan, and Trey all getting along, I realized everything worked out for the good. Middle school, here we come. I was super excited to be having a great day!

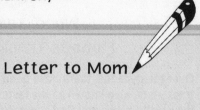

Letter to Mom

Dear Mom,

Learning the story of Moses opened my eyes to trust God to show me how to live and to lead. Dr. Richardson gave me high marks. My grades are excellent, and I plan to keep them that way. I've learned so much these last few years. I am worthy. I am capable. I can do all things through Christ who gives me strength. I know you're proud of me for graduating.

I'm also proud that you'll be on a new show that will be shooting here in Georgia. I love you and Dad so much. Antoine and I are at a better place too. Grandma is holding on, and Morgan forgives me. Wow, Mom, the Lord really knows how to work things out!

Your son,
Grateful Alec

Word Search:
Famous Track Players

Over the decades, there have been lots of famous and talented track stars, also known as the fastest men in the world. A few of the great runners are: Carl Lewis (USA) and Pietro Mennea (Italy) from the 80s, Michael Johnson (USA) and Donovan Bailey (USA) in the 90s. In the 2000s, Usain Bolt (Jamaica), Asafa Powell (Jamaica), and Tyson Gay (USA). Can you find their names?

```
F  N  Y  T  R  M  J  Y  L  R  R  L
W  U  E  S  E  H  H  R  L  N  N  R
L  O  A  N  S  S  V  K  B  V  H  V
V  L  N  R  J  I  W  B  D  T  T  R
F  E  E  L  C  W  E  D  L  G  A  Y
A  I  I  W  U  E  O  O  M  X  E  J
I  T  O  G  O  L  B  K  Y  B  Q  O
R  W  M  G  K  P  I  O  Z  P  T  H
H  X  X  X  V  O  N  S  R  M  N  N
O  A  E  I  Q  L  B  N  V  S  U  S
Y  E  L  I  A  B  V  O  A  Z  K  O
W  K  V  H  D  V  I  L  N  J  Q  N
```

BAILEY (Donovan)   **BOLT (Usain)**   **GAY (Tyson)**

JOHNSON (Michael)   **LEWIS (Carl)**   **MENNEA (Pietro)**   **POWELL (Asafa)**

TAKING THE LEAD

Stephanie Perry Moore & Derrick Moore
Discussion Questions

1. Alec London is not sure he wants to run for class president, but his friends think he should run. Do you feel he has what it takes to be the leader of the fifth-grade class? Name some qualities that others admire in you.

2. Tyrod brags that he can beat Alec racing. When Alec won, he didn't rub it in Tyrod's face. Do you think Alec handled the situation the right way? What is the best way to handle people who brag?

3. Alec is allowed to invite Trey and Zarick to a sleepover. When his friends don't get along, did Alec do the right thing when he tried to be a peacemaker? What are some ways to make sure you and your friends get along?

4. Antoine asks Alec to write a paper for him. Was Alec right or wrong when he didn't help his brother? What are some ways to make sure people don't get you to do something that is wrong?

5. When Alec gets frustrated with his life, he gets upset at the fifth-grade planning meeting. Was he wrong to walk out? What are some ways you can make sure you don't get upset with your friends?

6. When Alec overhears his parents arguing, he becomes worried. Do you think it was a good idea that Alec went and talked to his mom

about his concerns? Do you believe God hears your prayers and is always working things out for your good?

7. At the carnival, Tyrod is left out. Do you feel Alec did the right thing to have everyone include Tyrod in the fun? How can you be a leader at your school, on your sports teams, and at home?

Literary Terms

Literary Terms identify the different genres in literature. Here are some listed below and their definitions.

1. Allegory   An extended metaphor

2. Ballad   A narrative composition in rhythmic verse that tells a story

3. Drama   A literary composition involving conflict

4. Epic   A genre of classical poetry originating in Greece

5. Fable   A story that tells a lesson

6. Limerick   A funny little poem containing five lines

7. Ode   A poem about something the author is fond of

8. Rhyme   A repetition of similar sounds in two or more words

9. Satire   A work of literature that blends criticism with humor

10. Sonnet   A form of lyric poetry with 14 lines

1. An _____ is a poem dealing with what the author likes.

2. A _____ has 14 lines.

3. When a story tells a lesson, it is a _____.

4. If a story has conflict, it is a _____.

5. Blending humor and criticism is called a _____.

6. An_____ is similar to a metaphor.

7. A narrative song is also called a _____.

8. When words have the same sounds, they _____.

9. Poetry that originates in Greece is called an _____.

10. A five-line funny poem is a _____.

Math

Calculating the Perimeter of a Square

The perimeter of a square is the distance around the outside of the square. A square has four sides of equal length. The formula for finding the perimeter of a square is 4* (Length of a Side).

Example: | 5 | 4 * 5 = 20

Find the perimeter of the following squares

1) | 8 | _____   2) | 6 | _____   3) | 4 | _____

4) | 7 | _____   5) | 9 | _____

Calculating the Perimeter of a Rectangle

The perimeter of a rectangle is the distance around the outside of the rectangle. A rectangle has four sides with opposite sides being congruent. The formula for finding the perimeter is Side A + Side B + Side A + Side B. This could also be stated as 2*Side A + 2*Side B or 2*(Side A + Side B)

Example: 5 | 7 |
2*5 + 2*7 =   10 + 14 =   (Answer is = 24)

6) 4 | 5 | _____   7) 6 | 8 | _____

8) 3 | 7 | _____   9) 8 | 9 | _____

10) 9 | 10 | _____

137

Teach Me, Coach
Track & Field

It is exciting that you want to run and win the race. Well, you can sprint to it. However, there are a few simple rules you must know if you'd like to compete in track and field. Study them, and you will be ready for practice.

Basic Start and Finish Rules

Track and field start and finish rules are intended to provide audiences as well as competitors a definite sign of when a race has begun and ended. For sprinters and distance runners, each person gets an individual starting lane. Shorter races have the runners all line up beside each other. However, the longer races have staggered lanes to make it fair for additional circumference around the track.

A starting line is visibly marked and cannot be crossed until a starter gun is sounded. A runner can only have one false start. If a racer has two false starts, then he is disqualified from the race. The finish line is usually a line drawn on the ground as well as a piece of ribbon. The runner who is first to cross the line wins.

Can a runner have one false start? _____

Running the Race

In the races where the runners must stay in their lanes, each athlete must stay within his assigned lane from start to finish. However, where the runner only starts in a position, but can move over, the racers are free to merge later. If an athlete goes off of the track or steps on the line demarking the track, he is disqualified.

Also, any athlete who pushes or obstructs another athlete in a way that blocks his progress, should be disqualified from that event. However, if an athlete is forced by another person to go outside his lane, and if no advantage is increased, the athlete should not be disqualified.

In a short race, do runners have to stay in their assigned lanes?

_____

Basic Relay Race Rules

Basic relay race rules require athletes to use one type of baton during a race. Therefore, no grip tape or foreign material can be attached to the baton to give racers an unfair advantage during the race. If a team does not comply, they will be disqualified.

Another relay race rule includes the way in which racers get the baton from other runners. You are allowed to drop the baton, pick it up and continue your race. However, you cannot grab the baton from a racer at an illegal point during the race. If this is done, your team will be disqualified as well.

Can you use any baton you want? _____

Basic Shot Put Rules

Shot put is a track and field event that requires an athlete to thrust a heavy metal ball as far as the athlete can throw it away from his or her body. The distance is recorded and measured. The person who throws the shot put the farthest wins.

The shot put for a man must weigh 16 pounds. For a put to be legal, the athlete must place the ball against his neck and push it away from his body using only a hand. Competitors stand in a circle with a 7-foot radius. If the player crosses the line, he will be disqualified.

What must the weight be of a shot put thrown by a man? _____

Types of Track and Field Events

There are three categories; track events, field events, and combined events.

The exciting running events are categorized as sprints, middle- and long-distance events, relays, and hurdling. The tough jumping events include long jump, triple jump, high jump, and pole vault, while the most common throwing events are shot put, javelin, discus, and hammer. There are also combined events, such as heptathlon and decathlon, in which well-skilled athletes compete in a number of the above events.

What are the three categories of track and field? _____, _____, and _____

So those are the rules of the sport of track and field. Compete within the rules and challenge yourself to give a high-level performance. Remember to give your very best effort, and the results will take care of themselves. See you at the finish line!

Chapter 1 Solution

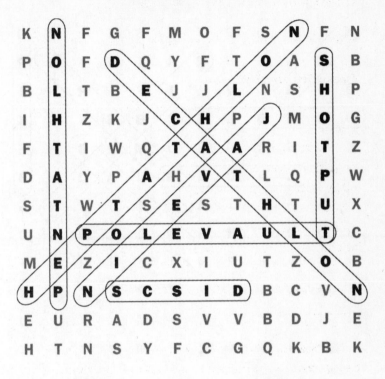

DECATHLON   **DISCS**   **HEPTATHLON**

JAVELIN   **PENTATHLON**   **POLE VAULT**

SHOT PUT

Chapter 2 Solution

```
N  T  Y  U  Q  T  K  S  I  L  C  S
I  U  L  G  H  R  A  T  M  K  S  P
Q  L  G  C  V  W  I  F  P  R  H  I
H  U  R  D  L  E  X  B  E  K  K  K
X  C  S  C  F  E  U  M  B  B  H  E
T  N  L  A  D  E  M  H  A  O  M  S
I  S  F  G  J  A  L  T  J  V  N  S
O  D  R  F  H  H  O  L  L  D  A  C
H  K  Y  H  F  N  J  E  J  U  O  F
T  D  W  J  L  E  Z  P  E  Y  A  R
N  K  K  M  S  K  Y  M  Z  V  I  U
A  P  S  Y  X  C  P  M  V  J  Y  L
```

BATON   GUN   HAMMERS

HURDLE   MEDAL   RIBBON   SPIKES

Chapter 3 Solution

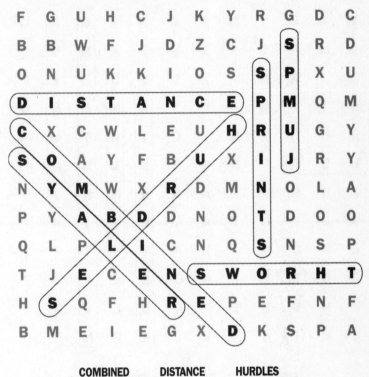

COMBINED   DISTANCE   HURDLES

JUMPS   RELAYS   SPRINTS   THROWS

Chapter 4 Solution

AUSTRALIA   FINLAND   GERMANY

GREAT BRITAIN   JAMAICA   KENYA   USA

Chapter 5 Solution

	V	W	O	S	E	I	M	P	U	D	V
Y											
S	I	Q	X	Z	T	F	O	B	S	X	P
H	R	M	A	S	A	X	E	T	L	K	S
M	G	B	D	Q	T	B	D	E	V	T	M
W	I	H	F	P	S	Z	V	A	A	A	Q
G	N	R	R	F	A	I	J	N	I	I	A
Q	I	Q	C	O	D	N	F	K	F	Z	R
F	A	W	H	A	I	O	O	K	N	N	B
I	T	W	N	B	R	S	S	Z	U	C	H
J	E	D	Y	D	O	O	H	Y	I	I	Q
T	C	P	K	W	L	G	B	H	M	R	H
I	H	Q	F	A	F	L	M	I	Z	T	A

ARIZONA   BYU   FLORIDASTATE

LSU   STANFORD   TEXAS AM   VIRGINIA TECH

Chapter 6 Solution

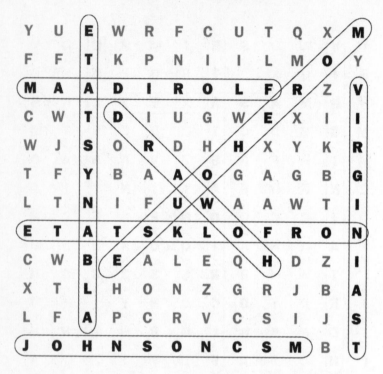

ALBANY STATE   **FLORIDA AM**   **HOWARD**

JOHNSON CSM   **MOREHOUSE**   **NORFOLK STATE**   **VIRGINIA ST**

Chapter 7 Solution

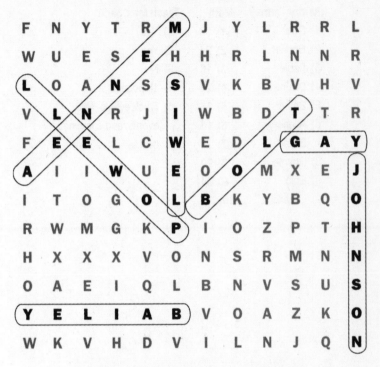

BAILEY (Donovan)   BOLT (Usain)   GAY (Tyson)

JOHNSON (Michael)   LEWIS (Carl)   MENNEA (Pietro)   POWELL (Asafa)

Answer Keys

Literary Terms	Math	Teach Me Coach
1) Ode	1) 32	1) Yes
2) Sonnet	2) 24	2) Yes
3) Fable	3) 16	3) No
4) Drama	4) 28	4) 16 pounds
5) Satire	5) 36	5) Track events, field
6) Allegory	6) 18	events, and combined
7) Ballad	7) 28	events
8) Rhyme	8) 20	
9) Epic	9) 34	
10) Limerick	10) 38	

ACKNOWLEDGMENTS

We've been making the climb lately. Not physically climbing a mountain, but actually teaching a leadership program to young people called C.L.I.M.B. The C.L.I.M.B. program stands for Championship Leadership Is My Behavior. A portion of this motivating series is woven into the story you have just read. The main point that we want to get across to our youth is, when you have the heart of a champion, work hard, and don't quit . . . you can reach your goals.

This premise is also a biblical one. The Bible teaches us that when you have a heart for God and put your trust in Him, He can do anything but fail. Therefore, we pray this novel touches the heart of everyone who reads it.

We have many to thank; especially our dear friends Antonio and Gloria London, their family, and Jay, their nephew, who inspired the main character's background.

To our parents, Dr. Franklin and Shirley Perry, and Ann

Redding, you all led us in our youth, and for that we are thankful.

To our Moody Team, especially Pam Pugh, Ed Santiago, and Janis Backing, you always take care of us and lead us in the right direction.

To our assistants, Alyxandra Pinkston, Alisha Torres, and Joy Spencer, you are future leaders, and we love watching you blossom.

To our friends who inspire us to be all we can be, Jay and Debbie Spencer, Randy Roberts, John Rainey, Peyton Day, Jim and Deen Sanders, Paul and Susan Johnson, Bobby and Sarah Lundy, Taylor Stewart, Chan and Laurie Gailey, Patrick and Krista Nix, Byron and Kim Johnson, Jenell Clark, Carol Hardy, Sid Callaway, Nicole Smith, Jackie Dixon, Harry and Torian Colon, Byron and Kim Forrest, Vickie Davis, Brock White, Jamell Meeks, Michele Jenkins, Thelma Day, Danny Buggs, Lois Barney, Veronica Evans, Sophia Nelson, Laurie Weaver, Byrant and Taiwanna Brown-Bolds, Donald and Deborah Bradley, Calvin Johnson, Tashard Choice, and Chett and Lakeba Williams, we are thrilled that you are there for us.

To our pastor and church family, Pastor Eric W. Lee and Springfield Baptist Church, you lead our hearts to stay focused on God, and we are grateful.

To our teens, Dustyn, Sydni, and Sheldyn, you give us the passion to lead in the area of writing uplifting books for youth, and we love you.

To our new young readers, you lead our drive to help

make an impact on the world, and we know you will become great at whatever you C.L.I.M.B. to do.

And to our Lord, You gave us the gift to write, and we pray You are pleased with how we are using our talents.

ALEC LONDON SERIES

978-0-8024-0411-4

978-0-8024-0410-7

978-0-8024-0412-1   978-0-8024-0414-5   978-0-8024-0413-8

The Alec London books are chapter books written for boys, 8–12 years old. Alec London is introduced in Stephanie Perry Moore's previously released series Morgan Love. In this new series, readers get a glimpse of Alec's life up close and personal. The series provides moral lessons that will aid in character development, teaching boys how to effectively deal with the various issues they face at this stage of life. The books will also help boys develop their English and math skills as they read through the stories and complete the entertaining and educational exercises provided at the end of each chapter and in the back of the book.

L E V B
LIFT EVERY VOICE BOOKS

LiftEveryVoiceBooks.com
MoodyPublishers.com

ALSO RANS SERIES

The Also Rans series is written for boys, ages 8-12. This series enourages youth, especially young boys, to give all they got in everything they do and never give up.

978-0-8024-2253-8

RUN, JEREMIAH, RUN

As a foster child, life for Jeremiah is a garbage bag filled with his things, a new school, and worst of all, finding a new family. Jeremiah holds on to his grandmother's promise of a handful of mustard seeds being planted one day to grow into a tree of his own. After being expelled from school again, he thinks that no one will want him to be a part of their family. With the help of his friends, he learns about teamwork and what it means to persevere.

978-0-8024-2259-0

COMING ACROSS JORDAN

When Jordan and brother Kevin decide to paint a mural (which is really graffiti) on the school's property, they get in trouble. They learn, along with their good friend Melanie, the lesson that even in using their talents to do something good, they have to pay attention and not break the rules.

L E V B
LIFT EVERY VOICE BOOKS

LiftEveryVoiceBooks.com
MoodyPublishers.com

MORGAN LOVE SERIES

978-0-8024-2263-7

978-0-8024-2264-4

978-0-8024-2267-5   978-0-8024-2266-8   978-0-8024-2265-1

The Morgan Love series is a chapter book series written for girls, 7–9 years old. The books provide moral lessons that will aid in character development. They will also help young girls develop their vocabulary, English, and math skills as they read through the stories and complete the entertaining and educational exercises provided at the end of each chapter and in the back of the book.

Lift Every Voice Books

Lift every voice and sing
Till earth and heaven ring,
Ring with the harmonies of Liberty;
Let our rejoicing rise
High as the listening skies,
Let it resound loud as the rolling sea.
Sing a song full of the faith that the dark past has taught us,
Sing a song full of the hope that the present has brought us,
Facing the rising sun of our new day begun
Let us march on till victory is won.

The Black National Anthem, written by James Weldon Johnson in 1900, captures the essence of Lift Every Voice Books. Lift Every Voice Books is an imprint of Moody Publishers that celebrates a rich culture and great heritage of faith, based on the foundation of eternal truth—God's Word. We endeavor to restore the fabric of the African-American soul and reclaim the indomitable spirit that kept our forefathers true to God in spite of insurmountable odds.

We are Lift Every Voice Books—Christ-centered books and resources for restoring the African-American soul.

For more information on other books and products
written and produced from a biblical perspective, go to
www.lifteveryvoicebooks.com or write to:

Lift Every Voice Books
820 N. LaSalle Boulevard
Chicago, IL 60610
www.lifteveryvoicebooks.com